D1625248

FAKESPEARE

STAR-CROSSED IN ROMEO AND JULIET

FAKESPEARE

STAR-CROSSED IN ROMEO AND JULIET

M.E. CASTLE
ILLUSTRATED BY DANIEL JENNEWEIN

NEW YORK

[Imprint]
MAKE YOUR MARK

A part of Macmillan Children's Publishing Group,
a division of Macmillan Publishing Group, LLC

FAKESPEARE: STAR-CROSSED IN ROMEO AND JULIET.
Copyright © 2017 Paper Lantern Lit. All rights reserved. Printed
in the United States of America by LSC Communications,
Harrisonburg, Virginia. For information, address
Imprint, 175 Fifth Avenue, New York, N.Y. 10010.

Library of Congress Cataloging-in-Publication Data is available.
ISBN 978-1-250-10162-4 (hardcover)
ISBN 978-1-250-10161-7 (ebook)

Our books may be purchased in bulk for promotional, educational,
or business use. Please contact your local bookseller or the Macmillan
Corporate and Premium Sales Department at (800) 221-7945 ext. 5442
or by e-mail at MacmillanSpecialMarkets@macmillan.com.

Imprint logo designed by Amanda Spielman
Illustrated by Daniel Jennewein

First Edition—2017

10 9 8 7 6 5 4 3 2 1

mackids.com

A binding ward this volume rings,
And any, be they serfs or kings,
Who touch its spine with thieving in their hearts
Will sorely whine with grieving from the smarts
Inflicted by its pages' stings.

FOR WOODY HOWARD.

Teacher, director, mentor, and friend.
Enjoy your well-deserved retirement.
Just not so much that you won't
come back and work with me again.

FAKESPEARE

STAR-CROSSED IN ROMEO AND JULIET

DEAR READER,

You are reading this because you expressed interest in the Get Lost Book Club.

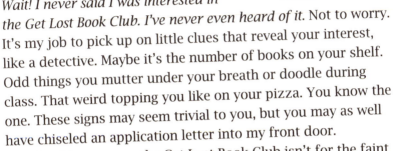

Now, I know you might be thinking, *Wait! I never said I was interested in the Get Lost Book Club. I've never even heard of it.* Not to worry. It's my job to pick up on little clues that reveal your interest, like a detective. Maybe it's the number of books on your shelf. Odd things you mutter under your breath or doodle during class. That weird topping you like on your pizza. You know the one. These signs may seem trivial to you, but you may as well have chiseled an application letter into my front door.

I should warn you, the Get Lost Book Club isn't for the faint of heart. Or the faint of brain.

We believe that the greatest power of a story is its ability to make the world around you go away for a while . . . and sometimes that "while" can be longer than you expected.

Intrigued? Worried? Downright terrified? You should be. Danger stalks these pages. Also, sword fights. Feuding families. Tight tights. Tomatoes.

Do you have what it takes to be a literary adventurer? *I think you do*, but it's up to you to prove it.

If, on the other hand, you want to turn back now, then no hard feelings. I'll understand. Some people just aren't cut out for thrilling chases, fascinating characters, devious villains, and a whole lot of fun.

But if you're ready for an adventure, step right up and follow me. It's time to get lost.

Go on, turn the page. I dare you.

Sincerely,

The Narrator

CHAPTER ONE
NOTHING GOOD COMES IN A BUCKET

Once upon a time, superheroes Mal and Cal Worthy were trapped in the belly of a yellow beast. The smell of salami was overpowering. Would anyone claw free of the monster's vile belly? Anyone? . . .

". . . Anyone?" the school bus driver called out again before shutting the doors. Immediately, two dozen kids began to shout.

Becca Deed covered her nose. Corey "Gorilla" Manila, an eighth grader about the size and smell of a sack of dirty elephant laundry, had obviously had salami—and maybe garlic—for lunch again.

Becca had been trying to escape into her brain, because her body sure wasn't going anywhere. The bus had been locked in traffic for an hour. She was a writer, and as such, she was the kind of girl who could sit quietly as she explored her imagination—but even *she* couldn't imagine away the toxic mix of eighth-grader breath.

She pinched her nose tighter. *Definitely* garlic.

Becca looked over to see her best friend, Kyle Word, snoring, his face pressed up against the window. Despite his last name, Kyle hated words and writing, but he and Becca got along because they both liked stories with epic adventures, dastardly villains, and justice for all. In fact, they were

5

working on a comic book series together, *The Astounding Adventures of Mal & Cal Worthy*, that had all those things. She handled the text while he illustrated—which was a good thing, because Becca was really only good at drawing a cartoon cat.

"Watch out for the Garblenuff," Kyle mumbled in his sleep.

"Wake up, Kyle," Becca said, poking him in the ribs. But his only response was to snore a little louder and say something that sounded kind of like, "I know karate."

Becca sighed. They had planned on plotting

the next Mal and Cal adventure on the bus, but Kyle had been tired all day because his little brother had woken him up extra-early. She guessed it didn't really matter anyway. It was impossible to focus on *anything* when surrounded by garlic-zilla fumes. Not to mention Kyle's sketchbook was still soggy from when someone had accidentally spilled tea on it. It had been a long day.

But one more stop and Becca would be home. And not a moment too soon, because, out of the corner of her eye, she saw Gorilla Manila dump a pack of itching powder down Kyle's shirt.

"Bye, Kyle," she said, standing up quickly as the school bus screeched to a halt. "I'll bring some aloe for you tomorrow. Maybe in the next issue, Mal and Cal should face down a bunch of giant mosquitoes."

"ZZhmm? What?" he said, waking up. "What do you mean?"

Becca knew the moment the powder met his skin. His eyes popped like a poked puffer fish and he shot straight up, scratching like a monkey with chicken pox. Or, since he was bobbing his head to reach his neck, more like a chicken with monkey pox.

The school bus's doors swung open, and she hurried down the aisle before Gorilla Manila dumped itching powder on *her* back. Eager to breathe clean air, she hopped down the steps—right into a tsunami!

Where had the water come from?

The last time Becca checked, she lived *miles* away from any ocean. And she didn't *think* it was supposed to rain today. . . . Maybe an elephant had escaped the city zoo and stepped on a water main?

Then her eyes cleared and she saw *the Bucket*.

The Bucket held by her stepbrother, Sam.

That bucket and the villainous smile on his face told her the whole story.

"Welcome home!" Sam said, his smile getting bigger.

"Welcome to your doom!" Becca shouted. Dropping her backpack on the sidewalk, she charged.

CHAPTER TWO
THE ONLY ANNOYING THING IS EVERYTHING

Chasing him wasn't really the best idea—Sam was built like a praying mantis, and when he wasn't sleeping, he was usually playing basketball. Actually, he probably played basketball even when he was sleeping, too. She was pretty sure she'd heard him calling out plays in between chain-saw snoring. The constant *thud-thud-thud-thudthudthudthud* of the ball being dribbled in the driveway when she was trying to write was the *least* of her worries, though.

Sam's dad and Becca's mom had been married less than a year, and she'd barely been able to tolerate having a stepfather, let alone the new "brother" he'd brought along with him.

Her stepfather was named Stephen R. Danielson III. He liked to say it *Three* instead of *The third*, for some reason. Becca guessed he must have thought it sounded cool. She also guessed that he'd never bothered asking anyone what *cool* meant.

SRD3, as his license plate said (ugh), was also a writer. He wrote copy for advertisements. When he found out she wrote, too, he'd tried to bond with her "writer to writer." Becca didn't see how selling people stuff with silly jokes was the same as telling beautiful stories about great heroes and brave adventurers. She certainly didn't think any of her characters would be caught dead saying, "Don't have time to dust? Dust to time, with the Tidy Tune musical duster! Keep on track with one step: a two-step!"

If Stephen R. Danielson III made her mom happy, that was great, but she wasn't interested in adopting a parent. However, at first she'd thought that adopting a *brother* might be better. That was, until she met Sam.

Obviously, she had been very, very wrong. Stepbrothers were no good, either.

"Just you wait until I get you!" she shouted as she sloshed across the yard.

"I don't know if I feel like waiting that long," Sam said. "The nursing home staff might not be happy with you tackling me in the pea soup line. I bet—*OOMPH!*"

"*Good* boy, Rufus!" Becca said as their new one-year-old "duppy" (too big to be a puppy, too silly to be a dog) viciously attacked Sam with his pink tongue.

"Gah! The smell! THE SMELL!" Sam gagged

as he got a whiff of puppy breath straight up the nose.

"Serves you right," Becca grumbled. An idea started brewing in her head for a new villain to fight Mal and Cal Worthy in the comic: Samoron the Worst. Or Samrog, Prince of Toads. Or Lord Samstank of Hoops. Becca liked that last one—authoritative, yet accurate. She just needed to write it down in her notebook before she forgot—

She stopped short. "Oh no! My *notebook*!"

Running back around to the front of the house and over to the sidewalk, she knelt down to examine her soaked backpack. She didn't just have schoolbooks in there—she also had her most precious possession: her ideas notebook. Dozens of story and character ideas had gone into it, and if the tsunami had damaged it, every good idea she'd had for the past three months would be gone.

Unzipping her backpack, she felt around inside. Dry. *Phew.* Luckily (and unluckily), her body had shielded her backpack from the water. It was only a little wet on the outside, and her notebook wasn't even damp. In fact, the only thing that seemed to have gotten truly soaked was a piece of paper in the outside pocket.

With her thumb and forefinger, Becca carefully pinched it out. At first she thought it was a spit wad from Gorilla Manila, but when she took a closer look, she realized it was even worse than that: It was a note from the public library!

A note that said three books were due today, and if she didn't return them, she'd owe $$$! *Triple* dollar signs!!!

Though the actual fee had been blurred by water, she was pretty sure the numbers would be the exact amount of change she had in her piggy bank . . . and the exact amount she needed for the entry fee for the Storyland Young Storyteller Contest, a writing competition that she and Kyle had entered. They had registered for the contest online, but they had to send the story and fee by mail, and the deadline to send them was tomorrow.

Becca was the sort of girl who splurged only once in a while, saving up for something she really, really wanted. Kyle, on the other hand, had a sweet tooth, and more often than not, he exchanged his coins for chocolate ones. He was getting his allowance tonight and putting some finishing touches on Mal and Cal, but if she didn't pay her half, their entry wouldn't count!

And that simply wasn't an option.

Because if they won, they'd get a free trip to Storyland, a new amusement park in Hawaii. Because they were only in fifth grade, they'd have to take at least one parent along, and Kyle had already said it could be Becca's mom, Jane. That was Part 1 of Becca's master plan.

Part 2 was that Kyle would go home by himself—she knew airlines let kids go alone sometimes when a parent okayed it—and she and her mom wouldn't go home at all. Ever.

No more Stephen R. Danielson III and no dribbling stepbrothers. She would miss Rufus, but she was sure Mom would book a cruise for Rufus to come to Hawaii after they'd found a house with a good backyard for him.

Swinging her backpack over her shoulders, Becca sprinted to the house. She always kept her library books on the shelf next to her bed, unless she was reading them or discussing story ideas with Kyle at his house.

Becca skidded to a stop.

She suddenly remembered that over the weekend, she'd gone to Kyle's house. They'd looked at her favorite comic series, *Rachel Never, Hero of No Time*, while eating Mrs. Word's cookies. In a chocolate-induced coma, she'd left the book in his living room.

"NoooooOOOoooo!" she yelled. Instinctively, she started chewing on a thumbnail that was already jagged from Sam-related stress. Her dream of replacing Sam and his father with white sand and flower necklaces was floating away.

"Becca?" Sam peered around the corner. Thanks to Rufus, he now looked just as wet as Becca did. "Why are you screaming—hey! Where are you going? Does Jane or Dad know?"

"No time, I'm on a mission," Becca called, wringing out her hair and marching off in the direction of Kyle's house. Her clothes were still damp, but this was more important than that.

"A mission?" Sam said, trailing behind. "For what?"

"My future!"

"WHO DARES CROSS INTO THE FIERY,
BOUNCY DOMAIN OF LORD SAMSTANK OF HOOPS?"
—THE ASTOUNDING ADVENTURES OF MAL & CAL WORTHY, ISSUE #12.

WORDS BY BECCA DEED, ILLUSTRATIONS BY KYLE WORD.

CHAPTER THREE
LIBRARY FINES AND MYSTERIOUS RHYMES

Becca glanced behind her as she marched. Sam was following, dribbling the whole time. Rufus lumbered along next to him, also dribbling.

"You're lucky I'm so fast," Sam said, dribbling between his legs. "I ran back home and told Dad you were marching off on your mission, and he said it was okay as long as I went with you."

He grinned evilly at her. "Don't worry, little

sister; I'll make sure you don't get up to any trouble."

"You're only one year older than me," Becca pointed out. "You're not my dad and *he* isn't my dad. I care about his permission about as much as I care about that squirrel's permission." She pointed at a fat gray squirrel in a nearby tree that was probably more fun to talk to than Stephen R. Danielson III.

She could practically hear her stepfather in her head. He'd probably said something like, *Don't be out too long! We'll wait for you, but dinner may not.* One of those lines that was *almost* clever or a joke.

And it wasn't like she was hitchhiking to another town. Kyle's house was only four doors down the street.

Sam tried to dribble once on each of the stepping-stones that made up the path to the Words' front door, but on the third one, he stumbled over his own shoelace and missed.

The ball careened into a bush and Sam careened after it . . . and Rufus careened after Sam.

"So mature," Becca muttered as she knocked. She knew boys weren't as mature as girls, but most of them didn't hit age four and then stay that way for the rest of their lives.

The door opened and Mrs. Word appeared in a flour-dusted apron. She was a professional baker and made the most delicious desserts imaginable—and probably unimaginable, too.

"Hi, Becca," she said. "Hi, Sam. Sorry it took a minute. Kyle must not have heard you."

"Thanks," Becca said, stepping inside. Only then did she realize what time it was—time for Kyle's favorite TV show. He wouldn't get up from *Allosaurus, MD* if an earthquake split the house in half, as long as he and the TV ended up in the same half. It was Kyle's absolute favorite show in the world.

"Hey, Mrs. W.," Sam said, "any chance there might be some baked goods that need testing? You know I'm happy to donate my taste buds to science."

"I'm sure we can find something for you to research," Mrs. Word said with a smile.

"I'll catch up in a sec," Sam said, and followed Mrs. Word into the kitchen, Rufus trotting at his heels and drooling slightly more than usual. Even though Becca was tempted by the delicious smells, she knew that cookies could wait. Her library fine couldn't.

But as soon as she walked into the living room, she knew something was wrong. Her writer's eye for detail instantly noticed three things:

1. Not only was the TV not on . . .
2. . . . but Kyle wasn't there.
3. And there was a backpack in the middle of the rug. A backpack with sparkly pink starfish stickers all over it.

Becca frowned. She'd know those stickers anywhere—

they belonged to Halley Pierce-Blossom,
Miss Know-It-All of Greenfield Elementary.
Those pink starfish stickers sat front and
center in class.

But what was her backpack doing *here*?

Becca and Halley got along okay, as long
as Halley talked about only one of the
documentaries she'd seen the night before
instead of all three. But Becca knew for sure—
as sure as the sky was blue—that Kyle and
Halley couldn't *stand* each other. Kyle had even
named one of the villains in the Worthy stories
the Vile Fanged Halleyodon after her.

"Weird," Becca muttered.

"Did foo thay thomething?" Sam asked as
he sauntered in with a full mouth and a plate
of slightly burned cookies. Rufus was orbiting

him, licking up any crumbs that dropped to the rug.

But Becca didn't bother to reply. She'd just spotted something else that didn't fit in Kyle's living room.

She pushed aside Halley's bag. Behind it was a small wooden crate filled with straw. The straw had a musty, oaky smell like it'd been sitting in the crate for years.

There was panting in Becca's ear, and she turned slightly to see Rufus's giant pink tongue next to her. She grabbed his collar before he could jump in like a five-year-old into a pile of leaves. Mrs. Word only reluctantly allowed him in the house at all after the Pudding Disaster.

"Could you hold Roo?" Becca asked Sam through gritted teeth. Rufus was just as much

Sam's responsibility as hers. Sam took one more bite of cookie, then reached for the dog.

Becca looked back at the box. In the middle of the straw was a giant book. Gold lines accented the dark leather cover. It looked like it belonged in the study of a haunted mansion.

Okay, this was definitely strange. The situation was getting less and less Kyle-like every second.

Sam picked the book up.

"Hey!" Becca protested. "You shouldn't have touched that—now your fingerprints are covering up those of whoever replaced Kyle's personality! Because that's the *only* explanation for Kyle to have this book."

Sam ignored her and flipped the book over. "It says *Romeo and Juliet*."

"I've heard of that. It's a—" Becca cut off as

she lunged after a now-free Rufus, who was wiggling toward the straw. "Sam, I told you to hold on to him!"

"*Romeo and Juliet* is a *loooove* story, you know," Sam said, batting his lashes. "Maybe Kyle got this for you, to show his truuue feelings."

"Don't be dumb," Becca said. "Though I guess that's like telling you not to be tall."

She tightened her grip on Rufus. "I was going to say it's a play by William Shakespeare. But the book must belong to Halley. Could you please just . . ."

She reached up with her free hand, but Sam lifted the book out of her grasp. "Kyle and Becca, sitting in a tree, K-I-S-S-I-N—"

"Put it down!"

Becca tried to keep Rufus still as she stretched for it, but Sam was just too tall. He opened to the first page, and a slip of paper fell out. She reached for it, but his basketball reflexes meant he nabbed it first.

"Well, maybe this is the clue we need," Sam said. "Finally the truth from ol' kissy-wissy Kyley Wyley, right, Rufus?"

Rufus barked once and wagged his tail harder.

"Stop that," Becca scolded her traitorous dog.

Sam looked down at the paper with evil delight, but as Becca watched, his expression changed to confusion.

"What is it?" she asked.

Frowning, Sam read out loud:

ENJOY YOUR
GET LOST BOOK CLUB
ADVENTURE!

Sincerely,

As pizza is more than just round, flat dough,

The tale inside is not just simple woe.

His family is her kin's ancient foe,

Yet you must get the lovers' love to flow.

Then read the final page to reach "The End,"

And soon enough, you will be home again.

"What does any of that mean?" she asked. It all sounded like gibberish.

"I don't know . . . ," Sam said. He riffled through the pages.

"Oh, so at last the big sixth grader doesn't understand something?" Becca asked. "But I thought you were soooooo old and wise."

"Give me a moment," he snapped, and ran his fingers through his hair. With his hair as short as it was, it looked more like he was trying to comb his brain back into place.

Still frowning, he turned to the first page. "It says *Prologue*—hey!" He looked up at her. "Maybe this actually has something to do with going pro! Did Kyle mention any interest in sports recently?"

Becca peered over his shoulder. "I think

prologue just means *the story before the story*. I've seen it in the front of comic books before. Regular books, too." For a moment, she wondered if she should quickly write a prologue to add to their Storyland submission. Maybe the story of how Mal and Cal first learned of their abilities . . .

Sam cleared his throat and read again, *"Prologue. Two households, both alike in dignity, in fair Verona where we lay our scene . . ."*

As Becca listened, Sam's voice got a weird echo to it, as though they were in a big marble hallway instead of in Kyle's living room. She shook her head. Maybe she'd gotten water in her ears after Sam drenched her.

Suddenly Sam's eyes bugged and he dropped the book. It hit the floor with a huge *thump*.

"What was that for?" Becca asked.

"It got too heavy!"

"What do you mea—?"

But when she took a second look, she saw exactly what he meant. The book on the floor was twice as big as she remembered it being just a few seconds ago. In another second it was twice as big as *that.*

Becca let go of Rufus, but for once the puppy didn't zip away—he seemed just as shocked as she was. Was Sam playing another prank on her?

The book was expanding outward before her eyes. The room shook. Rufus whined and hid behind Becca's legs as the book flipped open.

Chomp! Chompchompchomp!

The book snapped open and shut again and again, looking, Becca noticed with alarm, *hungry.* The room looked like it couldn't decide if it was melting into a puddle or crinkling up and blowing away. Suddenly the whole world was printed ink on paper, rushing and rushing around them.

Then everything went dark.

CHAPTER FOUR
ALOHA, VERONA

Becca lay on her back in the middle of a pile of straw, gasping for breath. She felt like she had been put in a tumble dryer and then pushed down a hill—a hill that happened to be the home of twenty scarecrows.

"Ppphuf!" she cried, spitting hay out of her mouth. "Ppphuf! Pphuf! Pphurf! *Blech!*"

The *blech* was in response to Rufus's long

pink tongue slurping across her face. He seemed thrilled that Becca was finally carrying sticks in her mouth.

She must have fallen asleep standing up and then toppled into the packing straw from the crate. That was the *only* explanation.

Next to her, Sam groaned.

Becca had to admit it was a little weird that he'd fallen asleep at the same time, too.

Carefully she sat up and took a look around. She leaped to her feet.

The room was gone.

Kyle's house was gone.

The whole neighborhood was gone.

In its place was a town square of old brick and cobblestones that looked like it belonged thousands of miles and at least five centuries away. Women in poufy dresses and men in tights walked in and out of stalls with signs that said things like FINEST BLACKSMYTHE, GIORGIO'S SHOE COTTAGE, and SALE! YE OLDE NEWE TOMATOES, BUY'ST ONE, GET'ST ONE FREE!

The straw she'd fallen into was part of a hay display according to the sign next to her, which read, FRESH HAY? YAY OR NAY? SURVEY OUR HAY DISPLAY ALL DAY!

"What happened?!" Becca asked as Sam sat up. His jaw dropped open as quickly as if someone had tied a bowling ball to it.

"Uh," he said, "uh, uh . . ."

"This better not be another one of your pranks!" Becca warned. "Because I really don't have time for it! The library closes at five on Tuesdays!"

Sam shook his head. "It's not! I promise!"

And he looked so worried, Becca actually believed him.

Sam reached for Rufus's collar, and Becca started to chew her thumbnail again. The last thing she remembered was the book coming toward her, its covers snapping like the jaws of a crocodile. But a book couldn't *actually* have eaten them . . . right?

Becca felt someone bump into her shoulder.

42

"You!" someone snarled. "Do you bite your thumb at me?"

Turning, she came face-to-face with a man dressed all in red except for a white lace ruff around his neck that made it look as if his head were being served on a plate.

Becca quickly removed her thumb. "Uh, no. I'm just biting my nails. I've been trying to break the habit."

The man frowned. "That sounds just like something a Montague would say!"

"A what-a-gyoo?" she asked.

The next second, the man reached to his side and withdrew a long saber. "Stand and draw, villain! *En garde!*"

Suddenly Becca was looking at the wrong end of a very angry steel blade.

Around them, the noise of the market

dropped away as everyone turned to watch.

"Hey!" Sam said. "What are you doing?"

Woof! Woof! Rufus barked.

Before the man could reply, a new voice shouted, "Do you quarrel, sir?"

Too scared to move her head, Becca jammed her eyeballs to the side, trying to see the new speaker. A man in a blue shirt walked up to them—he *also* had his saber out.

"Do *you* quarrel?" Red Shirt asked.

"No, I asked first," Blue Shirt responded, "so you have to answer first!"

"No, you do!"

"Excuse me," Becca said, keeping an eye on both their sabers. "I don't think any of you are a squirrel."

Both men looked at her in surprise.

"I didn't ask if he was a squirrel," Blue said. "I asked if this Capulet was quarreling!"

"Quarreling means arguing," Sam whispered loudly to Becca as he took a step back from the saber points. "And they were definitely arguing."

"See?" Blue looked triumphantly at Red. "You *were* quarreling—and now you'll pay for it!"

It was as if his words were a light switch.

One moment, the entire market was still, everyone going about their business, and the next, everyone in the town square drew out their weapons.

Before anyone got another word out, the whole town erupted into a colossal brawl, blue versus red, and in moments the shouts and clashing metal had Becca's ears ringing.

Becca looked at Sam.

Sam looked at Becca.

And for the first time in their lives, they agreed on something:

"RUN!"

CHAPTER FIVE
NO GREATER NARRATOR EVER SPOKE A PLAY...

Getting out was easier said than done.

With every step, Becca and Sam were almost knocked over as more and more people in blue and red rushed to join in. Rufus had to dance around like a cat chasing a laser pointer so that his tail wouldn't be trampled.

"Where do we go?" Becca shouted to Sam. "Now would be a good time to actually act like an older brother!"

"Uh, we need to hide?"

"I *know*," Becca shrieked. "But *where*?"

Suddenly there was a loud CRACKLE above them. Sam brightened up. "Maybe the thunderstorm will make everyone stop."

Becca frowned. The noise hadn't sounded like thunder. It seemed more like static on the radio, but maybe it was even more like the flip of a page from a very old, very dry book.

```
Becca and Sam knew they
needed to hide, and quickly!
Only the promise of a nearby
vegetable cart offered
some hope of protection.
```

Sam glanced over at Becca, who narrowly missed a flying tomato. "Did you just hear a loud voice say something about a vegetable cart?" he asked.

Becca nodded. The voice was strong, but not loud. Like someone sitting in an armchair at home, but somehow also all around them. Or as though someone had hooked up a microphone directly into their brains.

"Where did it come from—DUCK!" Becca shouted, and Sam dropped to his knees as a basket of tomatoes hurtled over him, barely missing his head.

```
If they did the sensible thing
and took cover in the vegetable
cart, maybe they'd have the
time to ask questions.
```

"Beats staying here!" Becca said, looking

around until she spotted an abandoned cart. "Go!" she ordered, pointing.

They raced through the battle, Becca using her backpack as a shield to protect them from flying tomatoes until they reached the safety of the cart. Rufus jumped behind it first, and Becca and Sam dived after him.

"Okay, who are you? And where are we?!" Sam shouted above the noise.

The Narrator, at your service. And if you'll allow me, I was just about to get back to narrating. *Ahem.* Becca and Sam were being given a crash course in the daily life of the Italian city of Verona.

Verona sounded familiar to Becca. Where had she heard that before?

Becca first heard about Verona when Sam read the prologue to *Romeo and Juliet* in Kyle's living room.

"Hey!" Becca protested. "Are you reading my mind?"

I am the Narrator. I know
everything. Like I was
saying, it was a beautiful
city and had been at the
top of *Best Home Pamphlet*'s
list of Places with the Best
Balconies for the fifth year
in a row, but alas, Verona
was now being torn apart.

Becca and Sam ducked another shower of
tomatoes.

"I don't know if it's being torn apart," Sam
muttered to Becca. "But it's certainly getting
sauced."

Pay attention, please! Verona

was being torn apart by two
families: the Blue Montagues
and the Scarlet Capulets. Both
claimed to make the world's
best pizza, and they had gone
to increasing lengths to prove
it. Now it was truly war.

Oh, and you may want to hold
your noses in a second.

Sam opened his mouth, but he suddenly
turned shamrock green. A second later, Becca
knew why. Well, actually, she *smelled* why.

A tall, skinny man in scarlet appeared in the
square, and it was like someone had liquefied
a flower garden and shot it through a hose into

53

Becca's nostrils. She could practically *see* the cologne waves rolling off him.

"Stand back, peasants!" he proclaimed, waving his sword dramatically.

"Tybalt has arrived!"

```
Yes, so that's Tybalt. And
he's the best swordsman in
Verona . . . but he also
has the worst temper. And
he doesn't like kids, so
stay out of his way.
```

Tybalt whirled his cloak, sending more waves of overpowering floral aroma toward Becca's nose, and she thought it would almost be worth sticking her fingers up her nostrils. Rufus whined loudly, and she quickly covered his snout with her hand.

"We've got to get out of here," Becca said. "Between that awful perfume and the swords and the tomatoes, we're going to get hurt!"

"If only I had a basketball," Sam said.

"For what?" Becca said. "I don't think your three-pointer skills are going to impress a crowd of bloodthirsty pizza chefs."

"Oh yeah?" Sam said, grabbing a handful of tomatoes from the back of the cart. He plucked one and rolled it around in his hand. "My teammates didn't nickname me Sam Kablam for nothing."

"That's a terrible nickname," Becca said automatically, though as Sam began to fire one red fruit bomb after the other, she couldn't help but be a tiny—a *teeny, tiny,* TEENSIEST—bit impressed.

His throws were fast, sharp, and accurate. One tomato even landed right on the point of a dagger and stuck there.

And then he made a mistake.

Tybalt staggered, and Becca saw what looked like a red sun splashed across his chest and face.

"Uh-oh," she murmured as Tybalt's neck swiveled around quicker than an owl's. His eyes locked on Sam.

"You," he snarled, and Becca saw he had unusually pointed teeth. "You owl-nosed, vegetable-hurling street weasel! You *ruined* my doublet!"

He swung his sword and charged toward them.

"What do we do?" Sam asked Becca.

She grabbed Rufus's collar. "We hide!"

CHAPTER SIX
BEWARE OF LOW-FLYING, BAD-SMELLING TYBALTS

Tybalt shot across the square like a mustached cannonball, while Sam and Becca turned and bolted. Rufus sped after them like a rocket.

Becca's lungs ached with the effort, and a stitch in her side began to pulse. She was good at writing chase scenes for *The Astounding Adventures of Mal & Cal Worthy*, but she'd never actually run for her life before. What if she tripped? The thought almost made her trip, and she realized she should stop asking questions.

"There!" Becca said to Sam, pointing at the open door of an empty shop. They dashed through, and Sam shoved the door closed behind them.

Tybalt's footsteps got louder, slapping on the cobblestones right outside the door—and then they kept on going, fading away.

Sam and Becca collapsed, leaning against the door. Rufus put his head in Sam's lap, panting like he had a tornado in his belly.

"Man," Sam said. "That was close."

"Too close," Becca agreed.

She looked around. The place clearly used to be a cheese shop. The air was ripe with the unmistakable smell. It had sunk into the wood and wasn't going anywhere anytime soon. The smell wasn't bad, but it did make Becca feel like she'd been rolled into the middle of a string-cheese stick. Rufus licked the shelves happily, leaving little puddles of drool as he went.

"What do we do now?" Sam asked.

Becca tugged at the straps of her backpack. "I don't know. You're the one who got us into this mess; why don't you tell me?"

Sam gaped at her. "What do you mean?!"

"You're the one who opened that book!" Becca crossed her arms. "I told you that you shouldn't have touched it."

Sam snorted. "Well, if Kyle just admitted he was in *wuuuuuvvvv* with you, we wouldn't be in this mess!"

"Ahem?"

Becca and Sam leaped to their feet as the
head of a boy poked out from behind a row of
shelves. He seemed older than Becca and Sam,
an eighth grader, perhaps. He had big, sad eyes

and just-too-long, messy hair. On his head was
a blue cap.

Becca and Sam shared a wary look. Blue
meant he was on one side of the pizza war—
what was it the Narrator had said? Blue
Montagues.

"If you don't mind, I'm trying to write," the
boy said. He scratched behind his ear with
a quill, and drops of ink splattered his neck.

"You're ruining my concentration. And your dog is slobbering on my boots."

"Oh," Sam said. "Sorry about that."

They hurried behind the shelves. It was clear that the boy had made this corner into his office. There was a little desk with a single rose in a vase. And there at the boy's feet was Rufus, eagerly sniffing his boots. Sam tried to tug the dog off the writer's feet, but the boy's feet must have been wonderfully stinky, because Rufus didn't budge.

Sam pulled one of Mrs. W.'s cookies from his pocket and threw it across the shop.

Rufus galloped after it.

"Excuse me," Becca said, "but could you maybe tell us—"

"Shh," the boy said. "I'm composing. I'm at a

crucial part of the poem. I'll be with you in just a minute."

"Oh," Becca said. "Composing, yes. Great."

```
After twiddling her thumbs
exactly thirty-three times,
Becca tried to think of
another way to interrupt
the poet without being rude.
But just as she was about to
ask again, Rufus began to
whine. Sam hurried across
to check on their puppy.
```

The boy didn't react. It seemed only Becca, Sam, and Rufus could hear the Narrator.

"Just hold on a second," Sam said, staying

still and crossing his arms. He addressed the empty space above his head. "Who gave you the right to tell us what to do?"

Stop that. This isn't a
conversation. This is
narration. Now then, Rufus's
whining was starting to get—

"Yeah?" Becca said, fists on her hips. "Maybe we'll just stand here and do nothing. What're you going to narrate then?"

Oh, I'm sorry, I thought
you wanted to go home.

Ahem.

Becca and Sam were silent
for a moment, as they soaked
in the truth that the
Narrator had delivered in
his rich, velvety voice.

"Okay, *that's* going a little far," Becca said as
the boy glared at her. He might not have been
able to hear the Narrator, but he could certainly
hear *her.*

She dropped her voice to a whisper. "But
yes, we *do* want to go home. It's not exactly
a Hawaiian luau being caught in a pizza war
because a book ate us."

Her mind clicked. "Wait a minute! If the
book is how we got here, maybe it's the way out,
too."

Now you're catching on.

You might want to *find*

that book and remember the

poem that came with it.

Rufus's whining got louder.

"How do we do that?" Sam asked.

BECCA AND SAM FOLLOWED

THE SOUND OF RUFUS'S

WHINING, CURIOUS ABOUT WHAT

THEIR DOG HAD FOUND.

"All right, no need to shout." Becca shrugged.
She and Sam walked over to Rufus, who was
cowering in front of a book.

And no wonder.

It was the copy of *Romeo and Juliet* that had eaten them! After what it had done—throwing them into an unknown land, subjecting Rufus to a world of tomatoes and nose-shattering cologne instead of tennis balls—his terror at seeing the book was hardly surprising.

"This is it!" Becca said, running forward to pick it up. Hastily she flipped through the book, but . . . "Sam! The poem! It's gone!"

"It's okay, Becca-breath," he said as he

grabbed Rufus by the scruff of the neck.
He took a deep breath, closed his eyes, and
recited:

> *As pizza is more than just round, flat dough,*
> > *The tale inside is not just simple woe.*
> > *His family is her kin's ancient foe,*
> *Yet you must get the lovers' love to flow.*
> *Then read the final page to reach "The End"*
> *And soon enough, you will be home again.*

Becca stared at him in amazement. Sam had
just recited something that didn't include the
phrases *pick and roll* or *fadeaway jumper.* She
didn't know what those were, but he seemed to
say them about four times a day.

"What?" Sam asked. "I have a good
memory!"

Or maybe he's a robot, Becca thought, but

she didn't say it out loud. Instead, she looked back at the book. "Okay, since reading the *first* line is what got us into this mess, maybe to go home, all we need to do is read the *last* line."

Sam picked up the book and tried to flip to the end, but it refused to open that far. The final pages stayed stuck together and wouldn't budge at any of his attempts to pry them apart.

"Let me try!" Becca said, grabbing the tome away from him, but it was no use. The last bunch of pages may as well have been a block of stone.

"Wait," Sam said. "Maybe there's a clue?"

Becca chewed on her lip, thinking. "Maybe . . . ," she said slowly. "What was the last part?"

"You mean, *And soon enough, you will be home again?*"

"No, before that."

"*Yet you must get the lovers' love to flow, then read the final page to reach 'The End.'*"

"That's it!" Becca said excitedly. "I think I know what the poem is saying. We need to make somebody fall in love, and once we do that, we should be able to open the book again and go home! And since this is *Romeo and Juliet*, they must be who we need to get to fall in love. Right?" She glanced upward, waiting for the Narrator to confirm.

She waited.

And waited.

And waited.

. . . .

Aren't you done waiting
yet? We can't move on
until you do something!

"So am I right?" Becca asked again.

It's not my job to tell you!
This is all about your journey.
It would be against the rules
of good narrative if I just
told you that you were right.

Becca smiled delightedly. "So I *am* right?"

Becca, who was a writer
herself, realized she should
not cheat her way out of the

```
well-paced story that the
Narrator was trying to tell.
It was time to get on with her
quest, especially now that
she knew what they must do.
```

"AHA!" Becca said, raising a fist in the air. "I knew it."

```
Curses.
```

"Okay," Sam said, "but how do we find these people? I knew a Juliet Miller in second grade, but I don't know where we can find a Juliet here. Or a Lame-o."

"Romeo," Becca corrected.

Sam shrugged. "What kind of name is Romeo, anyway?"

"Hmm?" said the boy, looking up from his desk. His hair stuck out at funny angles as though he'd been sitting there all week. "I'm sorry, have we met before?"

"Definitely not," Becca said. "Why?"

The boy raised an eyebrow. "Because you just said my name. I'm Romeo."

CHAPTER SEVEN
BOLDLY OUR HERO MOPES

"You're Romeo?" Becca said, trying to keep
the surprise out of her voice. After all, he was
so *small*. He didn't look like a main character.
He didn't look like someone who would bravely
ride into anywhere on a horse and defeat
whatever was keeping him away from his love.
He didn't even look like he could defeat a mild
cold.

The boy spread his arms dramatically. "Romeo Montague, at your service."

"Oh great," Sam said, quickly taking a step behind a cheese shelf. "Do you have a dagger, too?"

Romeo let out a sigh as long and gusty as a whale's good-bye. "I have only a quill and my sorrows."

"Er, that's good," Becca said, "because the other Montagues we met were pretty scary."

The boy looked insulted. "You don't have to be afraid of the Montagues. It's the Capulets you have to watch out for! They are the villains and thieves, after all. They're the ones who stole our cheese!"

Woof! Rufus barked excitedly, and Becca wondered how a dog who didn't know *sit* or *stay* understood the word *cheese*. Sam hurried over to Rufus and scratched him behind the ears until he quieted. After all, Tybalt could still be lurking.

"C-H-E-E-S-E?" she spelled out. Rufus stayed silent.

"Yes, chee—I mean," Romeo said with a glance at the dog, "C-H-E-E-S-E. The Capulets were jealous of our pizza, and to get back at us, they stole all of our mozzarella *and* our supersecret mozzarella recipe! We haven't been able to make a decent pizza since."

"That's awful," Sam said solemnly.

"It is," Romeo agreed. "Luckily, we've been able to come up with a new recipe for imitation mozzarella. We call it Lotsa-Rella. To celebrate, we're having a big ball tomorrow night. And that's where my sorrows come in." His face drooped. "I don't have a date for the party!"

Sam tilted his head. "Girls are a pain anyway. Can't you just go with some friends?"

"We are not," Becca said, even as Romeo shook his head.

"I can't show up to the party without a date. I'm Lord Montague's son! It would make the whole Montague family look bad if I showed up alone. Besides"—he sighed again—"there *is* a girl I'd really like to go with me."

Becca and Sam looked at each other excitedly. If Romeo were already in love with Juliet, it would be a piece of cake—or a slice of pizza—to get Juliet to love him back.

"I see her walk through the square every day, and I'm overwhelmed," Romeo continued. "It feels like—like, a . . . big . . . loving . . . thing."

Romeo sighed in frustration. "See? That's the problem. My friends suggested I write her a poem, but I'm awful at it! I've been taking a correspondence course taught by this girl

Ophelia in Denmark, You're a Poet, You Just Don't Know It, but it takes a long time for mail to travel between Denmark and Italy."

"Okay," Becca said, giving Rufus a scratch. "Maybe we can help. There's a type of poem called a haiku that might work. It's very short. Just three lines: five syllables, then seven, then five again." . . . She thought for a moment, then improvised:

> *She walks through the town*
> *Like music pattering in*
> *The minds of dancers.*

"That was a poem?" scoffed Romeo. "It didn't rhyme once."

"I agree," Sam said. "It barely even had a rhythm."

"It doesn't have to rhyme to be a poem,"

Becca protested. "There are lots of styles of poetry."

"Well, I don't think that's the style our new friend needs," Sam said. "If you want love poems, good rhymes are the seeds."

"Wow!" Romeo said as Becca rolled her eyes. It figured the spawn of Stephen R. Danielson III would come up with something so cheesy. "Can you do that again?"

"To win a heart, you need a brain. Just stick with us, and we'll explain!" Sam said.

Rufus wagged his tail. Romeo's quill quickly wrote down the rhyme, and Becca pulled Sam down to whisper, "This isn't a goofy game! We need this to work if we ever want to get home!"

"I'm getting him to trust us," Sam whispered back. "That's the most important thing. Once he agrees to follow our instructions, then we can figure out details."

Becca paused. To her complete and utter surprise, Sam was right.

"Well," Sam said to Romeo, "what do you think? I bet Juliet is going to love it!"

"This is great," Romeo said, turning to hunt down his crumpled poem. "But the love of my life isn't Juliet. Her name is Rosaline."

Becca's insides turned to Jell-O. "Are you sure her name is *Rosaline*?"

"Of course I am," Romeo said indignantly. "I might not be good at poems, but I do know people's names."

Becca and Sam looked at each
other in horror. Rosaline?

They had just helped Romeo
write a poem to the wrong
girl! And if they couldn't get
Romeo and Juliet together,
then they were doomed to stay
in Verona . . . forever.

"Thanks for reminding us," Sam muttered under his breath.

You're welcome.

CHAPTER EIGHT
ROMEO AND . . . ROSALINE?

"So what do we do now?" Sam asked.

Becca noticed his hands twitch, as though he were just longing for a basketball. She couldn't blame him. Only Rufus, who'd found a wooden spoon to chew on, seemed relaxed.

"Okay," she whispered. "We just need to keep him away from Rosaline until we find Juliet. And then we'll help him impress her."

"That's not a bad idea, Becca-breath," Sam said, and before she could tell him the rest of her plan, Sam snapped his fingers at Romeo. "We can help you get your dream date."

"How do we start?" Romeo said eagerly, folding up his crumpled poem and tucking it into a pocket.

"Like Coach always says: *practice*," Sam said.

"Exactly," Becca said, quickly stepping in before Sam started talking about dribbling drills. "You just need to learn a few good jokes and dance moves, and you'll be able to get Jul—I mean, Rosaline's, attention."

"And can we work on my poetry?" Romeo asked.

"Definitely," Sam said.

They heard voices and angry shouts from

outside the shop. Sam ducked behind a cheese shelf, and Becca dropped to the floor so no one could see her through the windows.

"But maybe we shouldn't practice here," she said nervously. "Some guy named Tybalt is looking for us."

Romeo's eyes widened. "You got on Tybalt Capulet's bad side?"

He let out a low whistle. "That's bad—really bad. Of all the Capulets, he's the worst. He doesn't just hate Montagues—he hates everyone and everything: rainbows, snow days, kids, and puppies. Especially puppies. They shed."

"Right," Becca said, picturing the shining needle point of Tybalt's sword. "Do you know a safer place?"

Romeo scratched his head with his quill. "I

think I can sneak you into Montague Mansion. We have plenty of spare rooms where we could practice."

Becca stood and carefully picked up the *Romeo and Juliet* book that Rufus had found and put it into her backpack. She made sure to carry the pack with both straps over her shoulders so they wouldn't lose it. The hungry book was their only way home.

Romeo opened the cheese-shop door and slowly peeked out. When the coast was clear, he nodded at Sam and Becca. The three of them sneaked into the street with Rufus tromping not so sneakily behind.

"Why do people keep staring at us?" Becca whispered.

"Probably because of your funny clothes," Romeo said.

She looked down at her outfit. "This is popular where we're from!"

"Well, it must be a place far away," Romeo said as he hopped over a pile of tomatoes. Rufus gobbled two, his cheeks puffing up like a chipmunk's, but nobody seemed to care.

"Why are there so many tomatoes lying around?" Sam asked as he stepped on one for a third time.

91

"Since we don't have any cheese, we don't need any pizza sauce, so the tomatoes that would have been used for that are going to waste," Romeo explained.

"But what about the Capulets?" Becca asked as she sidestepped a ketchup-y puddle. "Aren't they making pizza?"

Romeo blushed. "Er, well . . . the Montagues might have stolen the Capulets' dough recipe. But that's only because they stole our cheese recipe first!"

Sam looked horrified. "You're telling me there's no pizza? But this is Italy!"

"I know." Romeo shook his head. "It's a tragedy."

Rufus's nose twitched excitedly as they wound their way down the streets. Becca thought Verona, with its lack of indoor plumbing, smelled much more . . . interesting than her neighborhood.

Several splashes of color caught her eye. There were posters up on the street-facing walls of several buildings. She couldn't tell for what, but she could make out the word TONIGHT in great big letters, and a logo that looked like two *F*s and an *S*.

Romeo suddenly stopped. "Wait a second."

Turning his jacket inside out so the blue trim wouldn't show, he gestured to them to follow him to the opposite side of the street.

"That's the Capulet mansion," he whispered. "We'll have to pass right by it. Keep your heads down and be quiet."

"Hey, nice rhyme!" Sam said.

Romeo beamed.

Becca rolled her eyes and lowered her head, though she couldn't help but look at the mansion as they walked by. It was four stories tall, and a small army of workers carried huge bouquets of red flowers and scarlet streamers inside.

"It looks like they're planning a party," Sam said.

"They are," Romeo muttered, his eyes still on the cobblestones. "They're revealing their newest menu item tonight: Instead-Stix. It's their imitation pizza dough. They found out we were planning our Lotsa-Rella Ball for tomorrow, and they just *had* to beat us to it!"

Sam pointed to the guards stalking in front of the iron gate. "Are those people in silver dressed for the party?"

"No," Romeo whispered, and began to walk faster. "Those are guards. In armor. With very sharp spears. Hurry!"

Becca kept her eyes on her feet, trying to stay brave. She noted how her heart rattled inside her chest and how her ears suddenly seemed to pick up even the littlest noise. These details would all be great for the next astounding installment of *Mal & Cal Worthy.* In fact, maybe she'd slip one more description into their Storyland submission.

Provided, of course, that she got out of this book, made it to the library, and returned the library books in time so she could afford the contest entry fee.

"Okay, we've cleared the Capulets!" Romeo said, and Becca looked up. "We should be good from here on out—"

He was interrupted by a sound that came from behind. The *fshhhhhink!* of a sword being drawn. A gravelly voice followed it.

"Not another step, Montague."

CHAPTER NINE
DON'T TRICK-OR-TREAT AT THE OLD CAPULET HOUSE

When Mal and Cal Worthy were faced with certain capture, they'd turn invisible and climb away. Or trick their way out of the situation with smooth talk like they did in issue II. In one of Becca's favorite sequences, Mal and Cal escaped a rampaging giant by just vanishing to another century.

But Becca didn't exactly have those options.

The only things she had were a lovesick poet, a basketball-crazed stepbrother, and one very friendly dog.

"Roo," Becca said, "say hi!"

Woof! Woof! Rufus joyfully lunged himself onto their would-be attacker. When Becca finally thought it was safe to turn around, she saw that Rufus was on his hind legs, his front legs draped across a boy's shoulders as he wildly licked his face.

"AHH! Evil breath! ACHOO! And even eviler fur! AHH-CHOO! AHH-CHOO! AHH-OO!" The boy fell to the ground under Rufus's weight.

Becca, Sam, and Romeo hurried over to take a look at the guard.

He wasn't much older than they were, but a sword in a white leather scabbard hung on his belt and he was carrying a large, lumpy sack. His hair looked like he combed it with a thornbush.

"It's Mercutio!" Romeo said. "Call the dog off—he's a friend!"

Sam tugged on Roo's collar, but he seemed much more interested in tasting Mercutio's face than listening to Sam. Becca grabbed a bruised tomato from the ground. At least there was one good thing about the Pizza Feud: There were always tomatoes when you needed them.

"Hey, boy," she said, holding the fruit above Rufus's nose. "FETCH!"

She lobbed the tomato as far as she could. He tore after it, yapping excitedly.

"Not bad," Sam said. "You have a good arm."

Romeo helped the boy, Mercutio, up. His nose was red enough to match any Capulet outfit.

"Thanks," Mercutio said thickly. "I love dogs, but my nose and I really don't agree on that."

Romeo pulled out a handkerchief. "You scared us half to death," he said as Mercutio gratefully took the cloth.

"I would've gotten away with it," Mercutio said, wiping his nose. "But the dog ruined it!"

"This is my best friend, Mercutio," Romeo said, turning to Becca and Sam. "This is . . . I never actually got your names, did I?"

"I'm Becca," Becca said. "And this boy with the untied shoe is Sam. The dog is Rufus."

"Charmed," Mercutio said, energetically shaking Becca's and Sam's hands at the same time. He turned to Romeo and slapped him on the shoulder. "Romeo, madman, *lover* of good poetry and writer of . . . bad poetry. Best Friend, Confidant, Cool Dude, and my personal favorite—Partner in Pranks!"

"Pranks?" Becca looked at Romeo in surprise. With his sad expression, it was hard to picture him doing anything as fun as pranks.

"I know," Mercutio said, looking at Romeo with a shake of his head. "Hard to believe for somebody who just met him, I'm sure. Back in the day, Romeo was a master of practical jokes, pratfalls, goofs, gimmicks, and all kinds of nonsense. Once we tricked Lord Montague into gluing his hat to his own elbow!"

"Yes, it's true," Romeo said. "But that was when we were children—now I am a man in love!"

Becca felt the contents of her stomach swirl a bit, and from Sam's grimace, she knew he felt the same. Romeo was . . . a little dramatic.

"Er, right," Mercutio said, patting Romeo on the shoulder. "You are very grown-up now, *but*"—he wiggled his eyebrows—"wouldn't you like to do one last prank, just for old times' sake?"

"*I* would!" Sam said, but catching Becca's glare, he quickly added, "Er, maybe another time, though. We need to help Romeo practice for his date."

"Oh?" Mercutio looked at Romeo in surprise. "You got one?"

Romeo squirmed. "Well, not *exactly*, but Sam and Becca have promised to help me ask out Rosaline for tomorrow's Lotsa-Rella Ball."

Mercutio's face cracked into a wide grin. "This couldn't be more perfect! I'm going to sneak into the Capulets' party tonight. I'm planning a leeeetle prank of my own," he yelled. "You can help me *and* meet the love of your life."

"I doubt that," Becca said, hugging her backpack closer to her. Mercutio seemed like fun, but she needed Romeo to be focused. "Thanks for the offer, but we need to get going—"

"Tybalt and I have a score to settle," Mercutio interrupted, rubbing at his nose and sniffling.

"I'm sure you're wondering why I'm wearing only my *third*-favorite white silk jacket today."

"I was, actually," Romeo said.

"Of course!" Mercutio said. He sniffled again. "Who wouldn't?! That perfume-fountain and his nose caterpillar borrowed my first and second favorites, and he got them all slashed up in sword practice! Once I get my hands on— haaaaa, ahhhhh, HACHOOO!"

Rufus was back. He dropped the slobbery tomato at Becca's feet.

Woof! The tomato looked like it'd been in a game of catch between giant slugs. Trying to ignore the sticky saliva, she threw it again for him.

"Thank you." Mercutio sniffed, and the snot retreated back into his nose. "Anyways, as I was saying . . . Wanna sneak into the Instead-Stix party tonight?"

"Tempting, but"—Romeo looked sideways at Becca and Sam—"I need to see Rosaline."

"Didn't I say?" Mercutio blew his nose one last time. "Rosaline will be at the Instead-Stix party, too!"

Romeo lit up like a firefly.

"But—but—but," Sam sputtered. "You can't meet Rosaline until you practice!"

"We can practice at the party," Romeo said. "I *need* to see Rosaline!"

From the lovesick expression on his face, Becca knew they were in trouble.

"Then we'll go with you," she said quickly. If they went to the party, they could at least try to keep Romeo away from Rosaline until they found Juliet.

"Excellent!" Romeo said. "Party it is!"

"Wait a second," Sam said. "Aren't you forgetting something? Rosaline is going to be at a *Capulet* party—and you're a *Montague*."

Romeo's shoulders slumped like a bicycle tire with a hole. "Oh, right."

Becca began to nod her approval at Sam, but she quickly stopped herself. Sam already bragged enough. It was one of the reasons she wanted to escape to Hawaii with Mom.

"Never fear!" Mercutio said. "It's a

masquerade ball! Everyone must wear a mask. No one will recognize you." He straightened his sword belt. "Of course, it'll be harder to get *into* the party."

"What do you mean?" Becca asked. If it was impossible to get in, maybe there was still a chance they could persuade Romeo to skip the Capulets' party.

"I overheard the guards, and they said they will be checking the guests carefully to make sure that nothing funny—ha-ha-HACHOO! HACHOO!"

Becca glanced around to see Rufus galloping toward them, ears flapping. He skidded to a halt in front of her and deposited the contents of his mouth onto her foot.

It wasn't a tomato, but a rolled-up piece of

paper. Becca gingerly pinched it up. "This isn't what you were supposed to fetch," she said.

Woof! Woof!

Sam reached into his pockets and gave Rufus another cookie. "I've been trying to get him to fetch the newspaper in the morning," he said.

"But it's not a newspaper," Becca said. Looking at the wet paper more closely, she realized it was one of the posters she'd seen around the city.

PERFORMING TONIGHT AT
CAPULET MANSION:
MADAME LORELEI AND HER
FIERY-FOOTED STEEDS!
ENTERTAINMENT FOR ALL AGES,
OCCASIONS, AND TASTES!
MARVEL AT DRAMA, ACROBATICS,
MUSIC, AND NOVELTY ACTS

"Ooh, the FFS!" Mercutio said. "They're world famous for their impressions and avant-garde plays. If only I didn't have to avenge my best suit, I would probably stay at the party just to watch them perform."

The creaking and clip-clopping of a large wagon drew Becca's attention away from the poster. On the wagon's side was the same logo that was in the middle of the poster.

"I have an idea," she said, turning to the boys. "I hope you don't get stage fright!"

CHAPTER TEN
SOME POEMS ARE HAPPY AND SOME POEMS ARE SAD; SOME RHYMES ARE GOOD AND SOME RHYMES ARE LESS GOOD

"Excuse me!" Becca ran up to the wagon. The driver gathered the reins a bit, squinting like Becca was an unwelcome beam of harsh sunlight. Several men and women poked their heads up over the side of the wagon.

"We're new in town," Becca said, "but we're skilled entertainers, and we would like to join you! We are even willing to do our first show for free."

"Is that so?" the driver asked. "I'm sure you all did very well in your kindergarten production of *Counting to Ten: The Musical*, but I'll need a little more convincing than that. We require a recommendation for an audition."

"How's this for a recommendation?"

Mercutio said, strutting up next to Becca with a note in his hand. "A letter of approval from Lord Capulet himself. And since he's the one throwing the party you're performing at tonight . . ."

Lorelei looked over the note carefully. "Hmm, the note is rather short and hasty, but it does have the Capulet official stamp."

Mercutio winked over Lorelei's head at Becca and pulled a small metal object out of his pocket. A stamp. Maybe that's why they'd run into him by Capulet Mansion.

"Very well," Lorelei said. "I accept this recommendation. But you still have to audition. No favoritism in my Fiery Steeds!"

She pulled the cart into a dead-end alley, and her performers sprang to life.

"Steeds, assemble!" Lorelei cried. The troupe instantly formed a semicircle around Sam, Becca, Romeo, and Mercutio. Rufus had snapped the poster back from Becca and was gnawing it quietly at her feet.

"Now then," Lorelei went on, "we perform a variety of acts: musical, dramatical, comical, acrobatical, and so forth. But ants are banned," she said. "No ants of any kind are allowed to come within a hundred yards of the wagon."

"Aunts like in family, or ants like in bugs?" Sam asked.

"Bugs," Lorelei said with a shudder. "We, er, had a bad experience in Denmark." She changed the topic. "What are your skills? Are you musicians? Actors? Dancers?"

"None of the above," Becca said, and gently shoved Sam forward. "First, I present our athlete, Samstank—er, Sam Kablam!"

"Hey!" Sam said, looking back to glare at her.

Becca nodded at him. "You perform in front of gymfuls of people all the time!"

Sam crossed his eyes at her, but he said, "For this act, I will need a basketball."

There was an uneasy silence as the actors looked at Sam and at one another, trying to understand his words. Then one of them went into the cart and came back out with a round ball made of woven wicker.

Literally, a basket-ball.

The actor tossed it to Sam, who expertly caught it and instantly tried to bounce it. . . .

"TA-DA," HE SAID IN A VERY SMALL VOICE.

"Enough!" Lorelei said. "I think we've all seen quite enough. I don't care if you have a recommendation co-signed by the Nine Muses! You are *banned* from the Fiery Steeds!"

Becca was running out of ideas.

"Narrate for yourself," she muttered.

The actors were slowly climbing back into the cart. Once they were gone, that would be the end of the kids' chance at sneaking into the Instead-Stix party.

This should have been a good thing, since Becca and Sam didn't want to go to the Capulet party anyway, but Becca knew that Romeo was so desperate to see Rosaline that he would definitely try climbing the gate.

Then he'd be caught, and how could Juliet fall in love with Romeo if he was in jail?

Rufus's whine interrupted Becca's desperate thoughts. She looked over to see that he was rolling on the ground. The whine got higher and higher.

The fur around Rufus's mouth was stained pale red, and he had tomato seeds stuck in his teeth. With all the tomatoes lying around, he could've eaten a few dozen of them just since they'd left the cheese shop.

"Oh boy," she said under her breath. She'd seen these symptoms from Rufus before, and she knew what would happen next.

Rufus lurched to his feet and took one hesitant step before . . .

PPPPBBBTTTTT!

He released a fart that sounded like a bugle player getting punched in the stomach.

BUUUUUUURP!

A split second later, he unleashed a burp like a bullfrog being used as a croquet ball.

He spent the next ten seconds going fart, burp, fart, burp, one pushing him forward and the other pushing him backward.

PPPPBBBTTTTT!

BUUUUUUURP!

PPPPBBBTTTTT!

BUUUUUUURP!

PPPPPPPPPPBBBTTUU UUUUUUUUUUUUURP!

Finally, Rufus let out one last combination and then sighed.

His tail started wagging again, as though he hadn't even noticed he'd just made the whole alley smell like a vat of hundred-year-old tomato sauce.

"My."

Becca looked up to see Lorelei pinching her nose.

"My oh my!" A thin grin inched across the theater director's face. "That was the most ghastly performance I have ever seen! Your beast must be a part of the Fiery-Footed Steeds' act!"

"We're his handlers," Sam said, gesturing to himself and Becca. "Roo doesn't go anywhere without us."

Lorelei squinted her eyes, then nodded. "All right. But *you*," she said, pointing to Romeo, "still need to audition."

"Uh, yes," Romeo said. "I . . ."

"Read your poem," Sam whispered harshly.

Romeo gulped. "Of course. Just let me . . ." He shuffled through his pockets, little scraps of paper and empty ink pots spilling onto the street. He unfolded a scraggly old piece of parchment and cleared his throat:

My love is like a little bird
That sings at morning time.
The song it sings does sound absurd,
No melody or rhyme.
But what can I expect this bird
Who hops around, this little bird,
Wow, not much else that sounds like bird,
Or, for that matter, time.

The Fiery-Footed Steeds were starting to chuckle. Several amused snorts bubbled up. Romeo looked up nervously, then kept going:

This lovebird with its birdy love
Which fits it like a birdy glove . . .

Romeo paused, scratching the top of his

head with the quill nub. "Would birds wear gloves? Or three-toed shoes?" He looked helplessly out at the Steeds. "Bird clothing's not exactly my specialty."

The actors were now guffawing! Tears of laughter streamed down the troupe's faces.

"Maybe I should skip ahead," Romeo rambled, "and get back to the love part before I completely lose the rhyme. Oh, never mind."

"Bravo!" Lorelei said, as the rest of her actors hopped onto their feet for a standing ovation. "If you include this poem in your act, you'll be set for many years! It must be so hard for you to come up with words that rhyme so badly."

Romeo opened his mouth to protest, but Becca quickly stepped on his toe.

"You are welcome to go through the Fiery-Footed Steeds' costumes to figure out what you'll need for tonight," Lorelei said. "Let me have a word with your manager."

"Naturally," Mercutio said, sticking out his hand and smiling a teacher's pet smile. He stepped off to the side with Lorelei to look at some paperwork.

```
Even though the auditions
had turned out better
than expected, Becca
still had a strange
feeling in her stomach.
```

"Well, *now* I have a strange feeling," Becca groaned. And indeed, it felt as though there were giant moths wrestling in her stomach. They were now part of the troupe, but Becca *still* needed drop the books off at the library, do her homework, and work on her writing—all before bedtime!

"My stomach hurts, too," Sam said. "Can't you let us enjoy this moment for, you know, a moment?!"

```
Sure. Just try not to
think about really
sharp, pointy swords.
```

"Great," Becca said as she carefully checked her backpack to make sure the book—the only ticket home—was still there. "That definitely won't make me think about swords."

Happy to help.

CHAPTER ELEVEN
PRETEND PIZZA AND REAL SWORDS

"Hey, Becca-breath, what's smarter than a talking parrot?" Sam asked, smirking at Becca through his candy-cane-striped mask.

"Leave me alone, Samstank," Becca said. She looked miserably down at the parrot mask in her hands. It smelled like fifty years of book dust with a light touch of mold, but it was the only one that fit. Over her own clothing, she was wearing a long, feathery-patterned tunic in blues and oranges. Sam had found a jacket with bright red-and-white stripes that sort of matched his candy-cane mask and generally made him look like something you'd pick out of a bin in a drugstore for seventy-five cents.

Sam ignored her. "A spelling bee!"

Becca raised her eyebrows. "Yeah, well anything's smarter than a—a peppermint or whatever you're supposed to be." Sam just smirked and attached a lace ruff around Rufus's neck.

"Quiet back there!" Mercutio's head popped from behind the changing curtain. A large cape hung from his shoulders, and a gold crown was perched on his messy hair over his matching gold mask. "We're going to go through the gates soon, and we don't want any extra attention."

"Where did you get that?" Sam asked, looking at the crown in obvious jealousy. "It's way better than any of our hats."

Mercutio removed the crown and gave it an extra polish. "This old thing? Borrowed it from the prince of Denmark. Possibly without asking or telling him."

Becca narrowed her eyes at him. "You stole it," she said.

"You make it sound so . . . thief-ish," Mercutio said. "Besides, somebody's already stolen Hamlet's crown, metaphorically speak—Achoo!"

"What's Roo going to wear?" Becca wondered out loud. Tybalt had definitely seen their puppy with them. And if he disliked dogs because of their fur, what would he think of a dog like Rufus who could eat all the laundry AND bark AND shed?

A horn suddenly bellowed from the front of the cart. As they rolled to a stop, they heard Lorelei yell, "Steeds, *dismount!*"

"I guess this is it," Romeo said, looking around at Mercutio, Becca, Sam, and Rufus. He was wearing a sad-face mask that fit almost too perfectly. "Good luck!"

Sam gripped Rufus's lace ruff and followed a sneezing Mercutio out of the cart. Becca also made to go, but she glanced behind once last time. The straps of her purple backpack were tucked under a papier-mâché giraffe. She threw a scarf over it to make sure the bag and the book inside were completely hidden.

"Becca-breath, hurry up!"

Becca climbed out of the cart. The side entrance of Capulet Mansion wasn't as big as the main entrance, but it still loomed high over her head. Through the small eyeholes of her parrot mask, she could see a couple of bored-looking guards, and then a whiff of roses drenched in violet perfume mixed with an entire candle shop cut through the smell of her dusty beak.

Becca's stomach dropped as she turned her head to see the third person standing at the entrance: Tybalt Capulet.

He was in a fresh, clean outfit, but Becca

was pretty sure she could still see tomato seeds stuck in his hair from Sam's earlier attack. Her heart clenched. Tybalt might not recognize her and Sam, but how many people had a dog like Rufus?

Quickly Becca grabbed Mercutio's cape from his shoulders and dropped it on the puppy. Luckily it had two holes worn in it that went right over Roo's eyes. It wasn't much of a disguise, but she hoped Tybalt would think Rufus was just a very small child pretending to be a ghost for the party.

"Breathe through your mouth," Romeo whispered. "You won't smell the cologne as much, then."

"Just be casual," Mercutio added. "And try not to go totally nuts and flee at the thought of Tybalt's razor-sharp blade."

"You're worse than the Narrator," Sam grumbled.

"Who?" Romeo and Mercutio asked.

"Nothing," Sam said.

Becca tried not to stare as Lorelei spoke with Tybalt. It was hard to look away, though. His mustache wiggled up and down like a caterpillar on a bungee cord.

Suddenly Tybalt lifted his head and peered into the crowd of actors. For one heart-stopping moment, Becca thought she saw his eyes linger on cape-covered Rufus, but then he lifted his arm and waved them in.

It was only once they'd passed through the door that Becca realized she'd been holding her breath. She let it out slowly. Mal and Cal Worthy snuck into forbidden places all the time, and somehow they'd never fainted because they'd forgotten to breathe.

When they reached a second, bright red door, Mercutio swept them a deep bow. "Here's where I leave you," he said. "I must prepare my prank. Romeo, are *sure* you don't want to help?"

Becca looked at Romeo, who was standing on his tiptoes, his head turning back and forth like a sprinkler as he scanned the hallways for Rosaline. When Romeo didn't answer, Mercutio just shrugged. "Till later, then."

He took a few steps before calling back to them, "And watch out for Lord Capulet! He likes to yell at stuff."

"Stuff?" Becca asked.

"People. Plants. Baggage. He's not picky."

"Gotcha," Sam said.

"Also, the family nurse," Mercutio said. "She's old, but she has a sixth sense for trouble. And a seventh sense for hitting people with brooms."

Becca looked at Romeo and then Sam, who was struggling to keep Rufus back from the red door. From behind it, Becca could make out the sounds (and smells) of a party.

"Ready?" she asked.

They nodded, and she opened the door.

"Urp!" The masked man in front of Becca burped. Instead of looking horrified, the

woman he was talking with looked pleased.
And as Becca kept watching, she saw more and
more people burping.

And eating with their fingers.

And chewing with their mouths open.

It was even worse than the school cafeteria!

"Wow," she whispered to Romeo. "The
Capulets don't have any manners, do they?"

Romeo tilted his head. "What do you mean?
Everyone is burping."

"And that's
a *good* thing?"
Becca asked in
surprise.

"Of course!
If you like the
food, you're

supposed to burp." He shook his head. "The Instead-Stix must be an incredible success!"

Woof! Woof! Woof!

"I'm having some trouble," Sam said as Rufus strained toward a long banquet table covered in appetizers. "All this F-O-O-D is making Rufus hungry!"

Rufus whined and lunged forward. Sam winced. "If we don't find a leash soon, I think he'll yank out my arm."

Becca looked around and spotted several platters filled with what looked like thick, short ropes, each one about three feet long. She grabbed a few and knotted them together.

"Voilà!" she said as she tied one end to Rufus's collar. "A leash."

"Great," Sam said, looking relieved. "Is it also polite to provide short ropes to party guests?"

"Those aren't ropes," Romeo said, and pointed to a sign next to the platters:

INSTEAD-STIX

INSTEAD-STIX:
WHEN BREAD GETS NIXED,
WE'VE GOT YOUR FIX! NO RUSE,
NO TRICKS, JUST INSTEAD-STIX!

"*This* is what they want to replace pizza dough with?!" Becca asked. "Why is it so stringy?"

Sam poked at one. "Maybe it isn't so bad. Other people are eating them." He nibbled one corner, then put the Instead-Stix back down on the table. "Have you ever wondered what burned cardboard soaked in lemon juice and fish oil tastes like?"

Becca shook her head.

"Then don't eat this," Sam said. He was starting to look a little green. "Because that's exactly what Instead-Stix taste like. I hope the Montagues' Lotsa-Rella tastes better than this."

Romeo made a face. "Me, too! But nothing will taste good until I have a date to the party tomorrow night. We need to find Rosaline!"

Becca and Sam exchanged looks.

"Er, don't you want to practice what you'll say to her?" Becca asked.

"I guess." Romeo shrugged. "I was thinking of starting with something like . . . Look! What, er, good-lookingness—Wait, let me start over."

He cleared his throat. "You are . . . your nostrils are so cute—THERE SHE IS!" Romeo started flapping his hand like a fish out of water. "I SEE HER! ROSALINE! HEY, ROSALINE!"

Becca had never actually had an electric eel zap her right in the heart, but she imagined it felt the way she felt just then.

Halfway down a long banquet table stood a

tall girl with eyelashes as long as toothbrush bristles. She was *beautiful*.

Becca's electrified heart sank into her stomach.

They had already failed.

CHAPTER TWELVE
CROSSING THE ROSALINE

"Oh no," Sam whispered next to Becca. "What do we do?"

"I don't know," Becca said. "Think, think, think . . ."

"HEY, ROSALINE," Romeo called out again in a too-loud voice. He quickly pulled off his mask.

The beautiful girl smiled and walked toward them. But then . . .

. . . she glided right past them, without even saying a word!

"HI, ROSALINE!" Romeo said again, but he was still looking at the banquet table. Becca turned back toward the food, and for the first time she noticed the other girl who had been standing there.

This girl was stuffing her face with cinnamon Instead-Stix and tomato minimuffins. Her cheeks bulged like a hamster's when she finally looked up.

"Oh, hey," she said, her mouth still full. "Romeo Montague, right?"

"RIGHT!" Romeo said. "IT'S GOOD TO SEE YOU, ROSALINE."

Becca winced. Even though she didn't want Romeo to make a good impression on Rosaline, she realized that she and Sam would need to work extra-hard when they finally found Juliet.

Rosaline swallowed her mouthful. "You sound like a sick cow—do you always bellow?"

"UH," Romeo said, and then cleared his throat. "Uh, no, I don't," he said, this time in almost a whisper. "I didn't realize you were going to be here."

"Yeah, kinda boring, though. I was thinking of livening things up by 'accidentally' pushing Grandpa Capulet onto a cake or something." She guffawed loudly, and bits of tomato minimuffins flew out of her mouth.

"Oh," Romeo said, "I guess that would be . . . funny?"

"Not that you'd know funny if it came up and yelled, *Hi, I'm Funny* in your face." Rosaline snorted. "From what I've heard, you're a party pooper. You hanging out with circus freaks now?" she said, gesturing toward Becca, Sam, and Rufus without actually looking at them.

"Hey!" Becca said. "We're not freaks!"

"Sure you're not," Rosaline said, reaching for a platter of tomato cupcakes.

"For once, Becca is right," Sam said. "We're totally normal!"

But Rosaline didn't apologize. Instead she poured herself a goblet of tomato punch and began to gulp it down with loud slurps.

"Anyway," Romeo mumbled, "I was wondering . . . I don't have anyone to hang out with at the Montagues' Lotsa-Rella Ball tomorrow—"

"Oh yeah," Rosaline interrupted. "Hope that's fun. I'm going on a trip to Mantua to visit family. Ugh." She rolled her eyes. "I hope they all fall into a well before I get there."

If this party were a qualifier for the Worst Person Ever Olympics, Rosaline would've clinched a spot a few times over.

The girl smacked her lips and scarfed down

the last five tomato brownies in one bite. "Gotta go," she said. "They just put out the tomato juice fountain, and frankly, this conversation is boring."

And before any of them could say, *Good riddance!* she'd clomped off.

"You know what, Romeo?" Sam said. "I would send a letter to her family in Mantua thanking them for keeping her away from your family's party."

Romeo's shoulders slumped. "I knew people said Rosaline was hard to be friends with, but I thought maybe she was just misunderstood. That's why I wanted to ask her to the Lotsa-Rella Ball—I knew no one else had asked her yet."

For the first time, Becca felt bad for Romeo. She knew what it was like to hope one thing would happen and then have things turn out completely differently.

"Hey, man," Sam said. "You should give Rufus a squeeze. When I feel down, I find that a doggy hug always helps. Right, bud—RUFUS?!"

Sam was still holding the Instead-Stix leash, but the leash was no longer attached to Rufus. The only thing at the end of it was teeth marks.

Becca spun around, trying to locate their dog. "Look!" she cried.

Sam's eyes widened. "Not the punch!"

A girl was pouring herself a glass of what looked like lumpy tomato punch . . . and Rufus was running straight toward her. If he knocked the bowl over, that would definitely draw Tybalt's attention.

Becca had to admit that all Sam's basketball practice was paying off as he threw the Instead-Stix leash toward the charging dog. The makeshift lasso caught Rufus just in time to stop him from spilling the punch everywhere.

"I can't believe you were able to eat those Instead-Stix without getting sick," Sam said to Rufus as Becca caught up to her stepbrother and the dog.

"And I can't believe how fast and strong you are!" a girl's voice cooed.

Becca's head snapped up, and she saw a girl in a bright blue-white dress with a crescent-moon pattern batting her eyelashes at Sam while her matching crescent-moon headdress wobbled dangerously. "You saved my life!"

"Er, not really," Sam said, patting Rufus's head. "But I did probably save your dress from getting tomato stains."

The girl fluttered her eyelashes harder. "Like I said, you saved my life! Would you like to dance?"

Becca smirked as Sam shook his head. "Uh, maybe another time."

The girl's eyes turned sharklike. "I'm the host's daughter, so you don't have a choice." Her smile was sweetly threatening, or threateningly sweet; Becca wasn't sure.

```
Just when things seemed
to be getting better, who
should take a liking to
Sam but Juliet herself.
```

Becca's half heart attack came back in full force, and Sam's eyes became as round as marbles.

"J-Juliet?" Becca said under her breath. "Juliet is Lord *Capulet's* daughter? And she likes Sam?"

Yes, she is. And yes, she does.

CHAPTER THIRTEEN
SAM AND JULIET?

"This is bad, bad, bad, bad," Becca said. This was so typical of Sam—he was making everything worse!

Juliet was looking at him as if he were the last piece of apple pie on earth. Seriously, what could be more awful than someone having a crush on your stepbrother? Becca tried to rub her temples, but her hand just bounced off the parrot beak.

"Hold it!" Becca shouted. She marched between Sam and Juliet. "I'm afraid he can't dance with you, because . . . We are performers! And our performance is about to begin!"

She pulled Sam away from Juliet as fast as she could.

"It is?" Sam asked, following along.

"Yes!" Becca said with determination. "STEEDS, ASSEMBLE!"

```
Oh, I really don't know
if that's a good—
```

"*I SAID, ASSEMBLE!*" Becca repeated.

Well trained, the actors of the Fiery-Footed Steeds came running at Becca's call, including a very annoyed-looking Lorelei. "I said you could be *in* the group, not that you were now in *charge* of it," the director grumped.

"I'm sorry," Becca said, "but we have an entertainment emergency! Lord Capulet feels the evening isn't exciting enough. He sent his daughter, Juliet, to tell us to perform something."

Becca elbowed Sam and waved back at Juliet. She smiled and blew a kiss.

Sam turned red.

"Well, I suppose if the hosts demand it . . . ," Lorelei said. She quickly passed out scripts to everyone. Becca looked at the parchment.

Apparently she was playing somebody named Jolly Cabinet.

"Ladies and gentlemen!" Lorelei said, her voice cutting across the hall and hushing the crowd. "This evening, the Fiery-Footed Steeds proudly present . . . *Valona: A Tale of Two Delis.* Enter Rollyo!!"

The audience took a minute from burping to politely applaud as Romeo walked across the stage.

"Er, this city is a dump!" Romeo read from his script. "You know what it needs? Low-quality sandwiches. The Marliboo family will build a mediocre deli!"

An awful thought niggled in the back of Becca's mind as a few actors dressed in Montague/Marliboo blue entered the stage.

"We're going to break ground for a deli," Romeo announced to the new actors. "A deli that serves not-that-great, overpriced sandwiches to the unknowing people of Verona—er, I mean, Valona!"

Romeo's ears turned red and Becca's face fell. The play was a barely disguised tale of the Montague-Capulet pizza fight that made the Montagues look terrible. She hoped Romeo would be able to make it through to the end.

"Scene Two!" Lorelei called out, and two stagehands moved a table into place to be a deli counter. "You," she whispered at Becca. "You're Jolly Cabinet—you're up next!"

"This BLT is like a warm fire to my cold, hungry soul!" said an actor pretending to be a deli customer.

Becca quickly stepped onto the stage. "That's because we Cabinets are the best sandwich makers in the world," she read. "We're proud to help bring this city back from the brink of chaos."

Romeo/Rollyo appeared onstage again, and the audience booed. Even with the mask blocking his face, she could tell he was terrified. Beads of sweat dripped onto his neck. "What is the meaning of this?"

"You know what it is, Marliboo!" Becca replied. "Your family has been serving stale sandwiches! The people of Valona deserve better."

Romeo reached up quickly to adjust his mask. The sweat was making it slip and the string was loose—it was barely staying on his face! The show needed to end quickly, or else Rollyo would be exposed as the real-life Romeo Montague. From the hisses and boos of the audience, Becca knew they wouldn't be welcoming.

"Our deli was . . . was here first," Romeo read, pushing his mask up again, "and we'll see yours fall!"

"How about we settle this here and now?" Sam said, walking onto the stage. Lorelei had stuck a fake mustache on his mask that looked exactly like Tybalt's.

"I am Tabbert Cabinet and the best swordsman in Valona," Sam read. "And I challenge you to a duel!"

The crowd cheered loudly! Romeo's neck was now entirely covered in sweat. The mask suddenly slipped. . . .

"I have a better idea!" Becca said, ignoring Lorelei's glare. She grabbed a tomato from a nearby banquet table. "We'll win this fight the way we always planned—with food!"

She whipped back her arm and let the tomato fly!

It streaked through the air and hit Romeo right in the face—covering him with so much tomato juice that no one could recognize him even if the mask slipped more.

The crowd burst into uproarious applause!

Lorelei shrugged and motioned for the rest of the actors to take their bows.

The clapping went on and on.

Becca gave a shaky smile and bowed next to Sam. "Where's Rufus?" she whispered.

"Uh . . ."

Woof!

Rufus streaked from under a banquet table and ran toward the stage—straight toward Romeo.

In two quick bounds, the dog was on top of Romeo. Romeo tried to push him away, but he wasn't fast enough to stop Rufus's massive tongue from licking the tomato juice off his face . . .

. . . and his mask along with it.

Everyone in the entire hall stopped clapping and stared at Romeo. Including one set of very narrow, very mean, very cologne-y eyes.

From across the room, Tybalt unsheathed his sword. "THOSE AREN'T MARLIBOOS—THOSE ARE REAL MONTAGUES! *GET THEM!*"

CHAPTER FOURTEEN
A MARLIBOO BY ANY OTHER NAME

Everywhere Becca looked, there were Capulets running toward them. There was no way they could escape!

"RED RAIN!" Mercutio's voice bellowed from somewhere in the angry crowd.

It must have been a secret code, because several partygoers suddenly ducked under tables to reveal hidden stashes of tomatoes.

"Pour it on!" Mercutio shouted at his team of pranksters. Tomatoes flew everywhere!

171

Tybalt and the Capulets were caught completely off guard. Their charge toward Romeo was interrupted as the whole team of Montagues sprang out in a tomato ambush.

"Come on!" Becca said, grabbing Romeo and waving to Sam. "Let's find some cover!"

The three of them and Rufus dashed off the stage and came to a sliding halt under the nearest buffet table.

"I say we go out there and help Mercutio!"

Sam said, his eyes flashing the same way they always did before a basketball game.

"I say under this table is a great place to be," Romeo said. "Tybalt scares me."

Peering out from under the tablecloth, Becca watched Tybalt slice a flying tomato in half with one swipe. She couldn't exactly blame Romeo.

"But Mercutio's part of our team!" Sam said. "You guys can stay, but I'll see if I can get to him. I bet he has an escape plan."

Sam dashed out from under the table and joined the fray.

Watching him dodge flying tomatoes reminded Becca of when Mal and Cal Worthy accidentally dimension-warped into the middle of a meteor shower. Mal had had to do some fancy spaceship flying to avoid the missiles while Cal battled with the nefarious Professor Mackerel.

The Capulets fought back, throwing anything they could get their hands on. Tybalt directed a bunch of them to form a shield wall with dessert platters.

But no Capulet was as ferocious as Juliet Capulet.

She charged into the fight, as quick as a cobra. She caught tomatoes in midair and zinged

them back with a terrifying ferocity. As she fought, she spat a series of shrieking battle cries, comparing the Montagues to everything from disgusting swamp leeches to morning eye crust.

This was the kind of character Becca knew *had* to be in the next installment of *Mal & Cal Worthy*. Kyle would have a ton of fun drawing a warrior who could insult people until their heads exploded.

That is, he would if she ever got home again.

What had been a triumphant celebration had become an all-out battle. If Romeo hadn't been unmasked, Mercutio's pranks would have happened later and Romeo could have

```
met Juliet. If only Becca
had listened to the advice
of the very wise and very
helpful Narrator . . .
```

"Helpful?" Becca said. "You brought us here!"

"No, I didn't!" Romeo said. "This was Mercutio's idea!"

"I'm not talking to you," Becca said.

"Oh." Romeo looked around. "Who, uh . . ."

"It's not important," Becca said.

```
And now she was confusing a
main character, all because
of her sad frustration with—
```

"Don't you dare," Becca said. "You helped set all this up, and you're loving every second of it."

Well, who doesn't love a good
action scene? And that Juliet:
so ferocious! Boldly trying
to avenge her ruined party.

"Wait, that's it!" Becca said. She shook Romeo, who'd clamped both hands over his head.

"Huh?" he said. "Are we escaping now?"

"Not just yet," Becca said. "Do you see that girl? Juliet?" She pointed.

Romeo peeked out. "The girl wearing bright white, swinging Instead-Stix around like whips, and screaming at the top of her lungs? How could I not see her?"

"You still need a date for tomorrow," Becca said. "Juliet is smart and brave, *and* she's a Capulet, so you know nobody else has asked

her to a Montague party. Plus," she added as
Juliet tangled up one of Mercutio's pranksters
in an Instead-Stix and pulled him right off his
feet, "look how furious she is that Montagues
snuck into her party. Don't you think she'd love,
just *love*, the chance to get back at them by
sneaking into *their* party?"

She watched Romeo's face as he watched
Juliet. She could practically *see* him connecting
the dots.

"She's perfect," he breathed. "Unless she
murders me first because I'm a Montague."

"One problem at a time," Becca said
cheerfully. "Now let's go get you a date!"

CHAPTER FIFTEEN
PIZZA CHAIN OF COMMAND

"Come on," Becca whispered to a shaking Rufus. He was trembling so hard, the table that hid them shook, too.

It seemed there was a new (and only) food he didn't like: tomatoes.

"New plan!" Sam said, running back to the table as Becca helped Romeo and Rufus out from under it. "Mercutio's jumping around like a baboon on five espressos. I can't catch him, let alone talk to him. Oh, and when I say *new plan*, I mean that we need one, not that I have one."

"Not to worry!" Becca said. "I have one, and her name is Juliet."

Sam turned to look at the war queen Juliet had become.

"Really?" he said. "Is your plan to wait until she knocks down a wall so we can run through it?"

"No," Becca said. "My plan is that you can convince her to help us get away, and in the process, you can say something about how great Romeo is. Then we can start them talking!"

"Hey, Becca-breath! That's not bad, especially from a fifth grader like you," Sam said. "But what will we do with Romeo? I think we need to talk to her before she meets him."

Juliet's Instead-Stix whip cracked over the party.

"I'm okay hiding under the table until it's safe," Romeo said, and flung himself back under the buffet table.

"That settles that," Becca said. "Let's go!"

Sam led the way, hiding behind tables, statues, pillars, and decorations to get to Juliet near the main staircase. She was taking a short tomato juice break.

"Hey, Juliet?" Sam said.

Juliet whipped around, her eyes narrowed and her Instead-Stix raised. Her moon dress was shredded in places, and one sleeve was hanging by a single thread. Half her crescent-moon mask had been torn off, and the other half was barely on her face. But when she saw it was Sam, her face melted into a goopy grin. "Hellooooo," she cooed.

"Uh, hi," Sam said. "Great party, we're really enjoying it."

Juliet pouted. "It would have been better without those Montague fiends."

"Maybe," Sam said. "But I heard that Romeo came here to try to stop Mercutio."

Juliet's eyes narrowed. "Really?"

"Yeah," Becca joined in. "And now we *really* need to get out of here. Right, Sam?"

"Sam," Juliet said, smiling at him. "What a lovely name."

She picked up one of her Instead-Stix from the floor. "I'm afraid I'm not ready to leave just yet. I *refuse* to let this ambush ruin my party. It'll ruin my family's reputation!"

"*Reputation?*" Becca said. "What does reputation matter if—"

"What Becca means, er, sweet potato peel," Sam interrupted, "is that I got into a little argument with Tybalt. I don't think he likes your, um, Sammy Cakes much. In fact, he pretty much promised to shish-kebab me if he ever saw me again. So I really need your help."

Becca clutched her stomach. Throwing up now wouldn't help anything, even if Juliet was fluttering her eyelashes like a nervous butterfly.

"Samikins, don't you worry about a thing!"

She grabbed his hand and began to pull him after her. "Just follow me."

For a girl in a ball gown, she was surprisingly fast. Becca thought that if she went to Greenfield Elementary School, she'd have no trouble getting on the track team—or any other

sports team, by the easy way she dragged Sam after her.

As they ran up one of the broad marble staircases, Becca glanced back. Tybalt was slicing and dicing tomatoes with gusto. They were going to make it!

But at that moment, a red lollipop, probably tomato flavored, whizzed by Rufus's nose.

WOOF! WOOF!

Tybalt looked their way.

"Go!" Becca yelled. "He spotted us!"

Juliet took them through another doorway and up a smaller staircase, but Becca could hear Tybalt's footsteps echoing behind them, each one louder than the last.

Juliet flung open a big wooden door. As soon as they were all inside, she slammed it behind them, just missing Becca's tail feathers. The lock clicked shut.

Everything in the room was soft, bright reds, pinks, and purples. There were so many throw pillows and little blankets, it was hard to tell that the chairs and desks in the room weren't all tiny beds.

"Is this your room?" Becca asked, trying to picture the warrior girl she'd witnessed downstairs in this flouncy space.

"It is," Juliet said. "Nurse chose the decorations. She thought it'd make me more proper."

KNOCK KNOCK!

"OPEN UP!" Tybalt shouted. "I KNOW YOU'RE IN THERE!"

"Just a moment, cousin," Juliet called. Silently, she pointed to a pair of glass doors across the room. Becca and Sam darted through them and onto a balcony. There was just enough space for them to huddle in the corner without being seen from the room. And as long as Rufus was quiet, they would be fine.

Becca looked at her panting dog and wished she'd thought to bring Floppy Bear, Rufus's favorite toy. Then again, it wasn't like they had had time to do any planning before this trip.

She heard the door open, and a moment later a tidal wave of clashing flowers, mosses, and unidentifiable scents assaulted her nostrils. Quickly she covered Rufus's schnoz. It wasn't fair for him to have to deal with Tybalt's cologne again. After all, he wasn't the one who'd read the book!

"What's up?" they heard Juliet ask.

"I thought I saw those scentless scumbags enter your room," Tybalt snarled.

"Are you sure your cologne is safe to wear, Tybalt? It might be making you see things."

"I saw what I saw. There are Montagues in this room!" A strange swishing sound followed his words, and Becca couldn't quite place what it was.

Remember my comment about sharp, pointy swords?

190

Becca *wished* she didn't know what it was. Sam's fists clenched at his sides to stop his arms from shaking.

Juliet snorted. "I would never be friends with a Montague. I've never even spoken to one before!"

There was a huge pause. "Well, maybe they aren't Montagues, but they work for them—and that's almost as bad."

"I saw some suspicious-looking people," Juliet said. "But they ran off toward the East Wing, I think."

"Bunch of unperfumed, sparrow-brained, crumbly-castled cheese thieves!" Tybalt fumed.

"Put on some more cologne," Juliet suggested. "That always calms you down."

"It doesn't anymore," Tybalt said. "A key

ingredient in my signature scent was the delicate smell of fresh-baked pizza dough. But since the Montagues stole our dough recipe, I've had nothing to work with but flowers and tomato juice." He sighed. "The current cologne just isn't the same. See?"

There was a soft spritzing sound, and suddenly the fumes increased tenfold. Rufus let out a small whine.

"What was that?" Tybalt asked.

Becca quickly scratched Rufus behind the ears. Immediately the dog relaxed, leaning into her hand, his eyes closed in bliss.

"Just a bird," Juliet said. "The nightingale, probably."

"Maybe we should have a look," Tybalt replied.

The footsteps started again.

Becca and Sam looked at each other, eyes wide. There was nowhere to go but over the edge!

Ahem! If only Becca and Sam had seen countless action movies in which the heroes boldly dangle from a ledge for dear life when it seems all hope is lost . . .

Becca and Sam looked at each other and made a silent decision. Then, Sam grabbed Rufus, and all three of them swung over the stone railing.

Becca grasped Sam's ankle. It wasn't a long, long way, but if she fell, she'd still get

some pretty nasty bruises. Trying to remember Kyle's illustration of Mal and Cal Worthy hanging off an ice cliff, Becca braced her legs on the wall to help support her weight, and Sam adjusted his grip on Rufus.

"Shouldn't you be off looking for the intruders?" Juliet said loudly from inside the room.

"I am," Tybalt said.

The perfume got more

intense as Tybalt's party boots clicked on the tiled balcony.

"He's on the balcony!" Sam hissed. His head was barely below balcony level, and he had to duck to keep it out of sight.

"Get down and don't move!" Becca whisper-called back. "If we're still, he might not notice us."

She was sure the pounding of her heart would give them away. Her grip weakened. Sweat rolled down her forehead. But worst of all, Rufus's nose began to twitch. . . .

"I guess it *was* a bird," Tybalt finally said. The *click-clack*s retreated into the room, and then they heard the door slam shut.

"That was close," Sam said. "Let's get off of here before Ruf—"

ACH-WOOF!!!!!!

The shock of Rufus's sneeze propelled Sam right off the wall, and as he fell, his whirling arms took Becca with him.

So it wasn't pointy swords that would be the end of the story—just good old-fashioned gravity.

CHAPTER SIXTEEN
WINTER, SPRING, SUMMER, AND . . .

Arrrrooo

> *ooooooooo*

> > *oooooooooooo*

oooooooooooooo! Rufus howled as they plummeted. Becca curled herself up into a ball, hoping that would somehow cushion her.

Ka-THUD.

It seemed a springy bush worked almost as

well as a cushion. Becca twisted and turned, trying to free herself from the leafy branches all around her.

"That could've been worse," Sam said, pretzeling around to help Rufus up.

"And better," Becca pointed out. "If this bush wasn't here, we might all need body casts."

"But it was, and we don't," Sam said. "We're all doing the best we can. Especially poor Roo. Imagine the pain Tybalt must inflict on his extra-sensitive dog nose."

Becca tried to wriggle her way out of the shrub. The thick branches and leaves made it really hard to move at all.

The door to the balcony above opened again, and Becca stopped.

"Samikins?" Juliet said, poking her head over the balcony and peering into the darkness below.

If they were ever going to succeed at making Juliet even notice Romeo, let alone go to a dance with him, they needed to keep her away from Sam as much as possible. Becca put a finger to her lips, and Sam nodded. Juliet sighed and they heard her footsteps retreat. The door closed again.

"I hope Romeo made it out from the party without getting skewered," Becca said quietly.

"Just crushed," came a quieter voice from . . . underneath them.

"AHHH!" Becca and Sam scrambled out of the bush, and Romeo toppled out after them.

"Ow," he moaned.

No *wonder* the bush had been so cushiony. Romeo had leaves sticking out of his sleeves and tangled in his hair.

"Sorry!" Becca said. "You okay?"

"I'll survive this, but not my family's embarrassment," he said, pulling a leaf from his hair. "My only shot at getting a date for the dance tomorrow is a *Capulet*. And even if she does say yes, her sword-swinging cousin will stab me!"

"We can figure out what to do with Tybalt later," Sam said. "But Juliet's right up there—here's your chance to ask her!"

"I don't know. . . ."

"I'll help you!" Becca said. "I'm a writer—I'm good at writing things for people to say."

Romeo shrugged helplessly. "I guess I may as well try. It's not like I'll get another chance to walk into the Capulet mansion anytime soon. Especially after the, ah, tomato incident."

This was it. The last chance to return to their own world. If Becca and Sam messed up, they were doomed to live in Verona . . . forever. And

the way the feud was going,
they'd never eat pizza again.

"No pressure," Becca whispered grumpily.

I believe in you. That's
why I picked you.

"If by *picked* you mean *magically kidnapped into a city full of angry swordsmen.*"

Tomayto, tomahto.

CHAPTER SEVENTEEN
THE BALCONY SCENE*
*NOT ORIGINAL FLAVOR—NEW ZESTY RANCH

As Romeo prepared for the role of a lifetime, Becca and Sam held a whispered conference.

"You heard what the Narrator said," Sam said. "This is our last chance!"

Becca wrapped her arms around herself. "I heard. If this really is our last chance, we'll need to move quickly. Can you and Rufus get the book? It's in my backpack next to the papier-mâché giraffe in the FFS's cart."

"Why do you get to stay?" Sam asked. "I'm the one who's good at poetry."

"Because it was my idea!" Becca said. "And you're a faster runner than me."

"True," Sam said with a grin. He took off, Rufus following close behind.

Romeo carefully pulled the sticks and leaves out of his hair and clothing. He smoothed his hair down with his hand and did his best to straighten up his posture.

"You're looking sharp," Becca said to Romeo.

"Thanks," Romeo said. "I've never been a spiffy dresser like Tybalt."

"At least you don't smell like a fire hose of spoiled vegetable soup hit you," she said. "And even after falling into a bush, your clothes still aren't as wild as Mercutio's. I hope he made it out of there okay."

"I wouldn't worry," Romeo said, and brushed straggling plant bits from his doublet. "Mercutio's got a knack for slipping out of dangerous places. Me, though, not so much." He looked up at the balcony and took a deep breath.

"I've got you, Romeo," Becca said. "I'll stay hidden down here and help you out."

Romeo didn't say anything, but he flashed her a weak smile.

The balcony stuck out a little bit from the side of the house, and Romeo took his place underneath it. Becca slowly crawled her way back into the bush, trying not to get her eyes jabbed out by friendly twigs.

"Okay," she said as she picked up some pebbles. "Time to get Juliet's attention."

She hurled a pebble at Juliet's window . . .

. . . but it fell several inches short.

"Air ball," she muttered under her breath. This was when basketball skills finally *would* have come in handy.

Taking aim again, she thought of how Sam had focused on his target, be it Capulet, Montague, or basketball hoop. She drew back her arm, and . . . *Ker-PLUNK*!

"Ow!" A second later, Juliet appeared on the balcony, rubbing her head. "What was that for?" she demanded. "Who's there?" She had changed out of her mostly destroyed moon dress into a bright orange-gold dress with a sun pattern. A matching mask hung around her neck.

The torches hadn't been lit outside, so it was too dark for Juliet to see Becca and Romeo. It was now or never!

"Um, hi there," Romeo said.

"Who are you?" Juliet demanded. "Why'd you throw a pebble into my window?"

"What do I say?" he whispered to Becca.

Her mind scrambled, but for some reason the words that came easily when writing *Mal & Cal Worthy* in her notebook or on a laptop weren't coming to her.

Then, out of the darkness that had clutched her brain, words emerged. Bright, shiny, really lame words. The kind of words that were designed specifically to get into your head and never, ever leave, no matter how much you might want them to.

Ad copy.

Specifically, Stephen R. Danielson III's ad copy.

Becca leaned toward Romeo and whispered something into his ear.

"Hello?" Juliet leaned out the window. "Did you hear me? Stop throwing pebbles."

"A pebble now to avoid a boulder tomorrow!" Romeo said after Becca nudged him. "I'm the last one you'd expect to see, but I'm the first choice for getting you what you need!"

Becca held her breath during a long pause, waiting for the balcony doors to slam closed.

"Go on," Juliet said warily.

"Are you feeling run-down?" Romeo repeated after Becca. "Let down? Put down? Here's something that can get you right back on your feet, out the door, and in the mix: Revenge™."

"How do you suggest I get my revenge on the Montagues?" Juliet said. "And what can you, mysterious voice from the garden, do to help?"

"One bad turn deserves another," Romeo said quickly. "And where do turns matter? *Dancing.* Specifically, at the Montagues' Lotsa-Rella Ball."

"The one tomorrow night?" Juliet asked, leaning over the edge on her elbow.

"That's the ticket," Romeo said. "Or should

I say, *this* is the ticket. One all-expenses-paid-general-admission ticket to payback."

There was another long silence.

"Tempting," Juliet said, "and I like your style. But I'm afraid I'll have to decline. You should go back to the party and enjoy the Instead-Stix pizza." She turned to go inside.

Becca's mind was all sirens and flashing lights. Juliet was leaving! They'd failed! She tried to come up with more words, but before she could, Romeo spoke.

"I understand," he said, nodding sadly. "I'll pass on the party, though, because, well, it's a little embarrassing to admit, but I don't really like pizza that much."

Juliet stopped in her tracks and slowly turned around. Her face was red, and Becca wondered how Romeo could be so silly as to insult *pizza* in front of the daughter of one of the most famous pizza chefs in Verona. She braced herself for Juliet's explosion.

"Really?" Juliet finally gasped out. "You, too? Because *I* hate pizza!"

Now it was Romeo's turn to gasp. "Wow! I thought I was the only one. Pizza is just so, so . . ."

"Cheesy," they both said at the same time.

"Exactly!" Juliet said. "I've always been more of a sauce person."

Becca was shocked. She'd never heard of

anyone not liking pizza, but here were Romeo and Juliet, and they couldn't stop talking.

"Me, too," Romeo said. "I am a saucy boy, through and through. That's why I prefer pasta. Nothing wrong with a little cheese on your pasta—"

"—but it doesn't totally drown out the other flavors!" Juliet said, beaming.

```
Romeo and Juliet were bonding!
Becca didn't really understand
how it had happened, but
either way, she was ecstatic.
```

"I am?" Becca said. "I haven't been scuffing across a carpet or anything."

Not *static*. *Ecstatic*. It means really happy.

"Of course I am!" Becca exclaimed. "Juliet's talking to Romeo!" She clamped her hands over her mouth—she realized her mistake too late!

"Wait," Juliet said. "Romeo? Romeo *Montague*?" Her smile disappeared quicker than an ice cube in a fire. "You ruined my party!"

"No!" Romeo said. "Well, maybe, but I didn't mean to!"

"Oh yeah?" she glowered. "Why should I believe you?"

It was all falling apart!

"Stop!" Becca shouted. "Please! This was all going so well. Don't ruin it all now!"

Loud footsteps interrupted them.

Becca crouched closer to the ground, hoping the Capulet guards hadn't spotted her. But the figure seemed too short to be a guard. . . .

"Sam!" Becca said. "Did you get the—" She stopped short.

It was Sam, but it was *just* Sam.

No backpack.

No Rufus.

"Don't . . . be . . . mad," he gasped, clutching his side. "I . . . got . . . the bag, but then . . . I put . . . it down to . . . tie . . . my shoes. When I . . . turned around . . . there was only this."

He held out a little piece of paper, and Becca grabbed it from him. And as she read it, she felt like a pointy sword had been jabbed right into her belly button.

*I have your strange satchel and your
soggy-mouthed dog. You may have them
back on two conditions:*

*1. The Montague family must
return our dough recipe
immediately.*

*2. The prince of Verona must
appoint me as his heir, then retire,
effective immediately. Prince
Tybalt sounds nice, don't you
think? With me in charge, my
perfume empire can spread across
the globe.*

*If these demands aren't met, every gutter
and well in Verona will run red with
my latest masterpiece, Eau de Rotten
Tomateau. You will suffocate horribly,*

and you'll never see your dear pooch
again.
Most sincerely yours,
Tybalt Capulet, Certified Perfumer

CHAPTER EIGHTEEN
FOLLOW THE SLOBBER TRAIL?

The Narrator's page-turning noise rushed into the scared silence.

They had seen what Tybalt was capable of. He was willing to kidnap an innocent dog and threaten a whole city just to be able to wear his favorite

```
perfume again. If Tybalt became
Verona's ruler, no one would
be safe. Not even Kyle and
Halley in Hamlet's Elsinore.
```

"What?!" Becca gasped. "Kyle and Halley are trapped in a bookworld, too?"

```
Oops. Forgot you were listening.
```

"Are they okay—"

A crashing *thump* interrupted their conversation. Becca whirled around to see that Juliet had jumped off the balcony and into the bush. She looked like a furious windstorm as she shook her finger at Romeo.

"Our family is built on that dough!" she

said. "We're on the verge of losing everything without it!"

"What do you think losing our cheese has done to us?" Romeo said. For once he didn't look sad. He looked angry. "The Montague fortune is already melting away!"

"That's not our problem!" Juliet shouted.

"Not your problem?" Romeo shouted back. "Your family stole our cheese!"

Juliet blinked in surprise. "We did not," she said.

"Hang on," Becca said, stepping between them. "Is that really true, Juliet? Did the Capulets not steal the Montague cheese?"

"Of course not," Juliet snapped. "Our pizza's better. We don't need to cheat and steal to win." She narrowed her eyes at Romeo. "I demand our dough recipe back."

"I didn't take it," Romeo said. His eyes turned to the night sky in thought. "Now that I think of it, nobody in my family *actually* claimed credit for the theft."

"Wait," Becca said. "Are you saying the

Montagues didn't steal from the Capulets, either?"

"I'd just assumed it was us," Romeo said, shrugging.

"You expect me to believe that?" Juliet said.

"Like I should believe *you*," Romeo said.

The bickering started again.

"OKAY," Sam suddenly burst out. He'd been quiet ever since Becca read the note aloud. "Juliet, Romeo, you can sort out your own problems later. Rufus is in danger!"

Becca knew he was right. Even if they could get Juliet to fall in love with Romeo, what was the point of going home if they'd lost Rufus? They couldn't leave him behind in this pizza-less place.

"Sorry," Romeo and Juliet both mumbled.

"That's more like it." Becca nodded. "Juliet, Tybalt's your cousin. Do you have any idea where he might be hiding?"

Juliet shook out her dress, thinking. "He's been renting a room in the apothecary's shop. He's been working on new perfumes and colognes ever since the Montagues took our dough recipe."

"Except we didn't," Romeo said.

"Well, we didn't take your cheese, either," Juliet said.

"FOCUS," Becca said, pushing them both toward the front gate.

They walked in silence, though Becca was pretty sure she still heard Juliet and Romeo muttering insults to each other.

Better to be a friend than to fight again!

Stephen R. Danielson III's voice popped into Becca's head. It was what he'd told Becca and Sam during their most recent argument. She almost stopped walking.

Romeo and Juliet were annoying, but she and Sam fought just as much. Were they this awful to each other?

She snuck a glance at her stepbrother. His shoelaces had been quadruple-knotted and his head hung down. He really loved Rufus and always made sure the water in his bowl was fresh. He was actually kind of thoughtful, now that she stopped to think about it. He'd surprised her with his poetry, and she appreciated how much he liked words. Could it be that she and Sam were actually more similar than she had thought?

Becca reached out and tapped his shoulder. "It's going to be all right."

"It's all my fault," he said miserably. "I let Tybalt steal Rufus and the book. If I'd just tied my laces earlier, this wouldn't have happened!"

"Tybalt has a sword," Becca said. "He would have found a way to get them no matter what. But now we have a plan, and we're going to save them! We've already survived tomato bombs and Instead-Stix. We can do this, too!"

Sam gave her a small smile. "Anything for Roo."

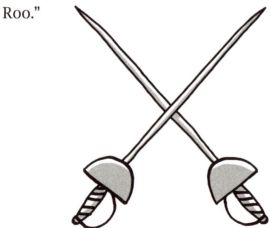

Instead of rolling her eyes at his rhyme, Becca smiled. "For Roo," she agreed, feeling lighter than she had in a while.

When they reached the gate, however, she felt her good mood disappear. She'd forgotten about the guards.

"What do we do?" Romeo whispered, eyeing their crossbows and spears, but Juliet kept walking with her head high. The guards snapped to attention, opened the gate, and let them all pass without a word.

She wore confidence like a suit of armor. The line drifted into Becca's mind, and she made a mental note to include it in the next *Mal & Cal Worthy* comic book. With that kind of writing, she and Kyle could definitely win the trip to Hawaii! But maybe—just *maybe*—she and her mother didn't have to stay there forever.

"Which way to the apothecary?" Sam whispered.

"North," Juliet said.

"South," Romeo said.

"Wrong!"

They all jumped at the sound of a *fourth* voice. As Juliet stepped back, she hit a tree root and tumbled to the ground.

"How long have you been there?" Becca asked.

"Long enough to know what's happened." Mercutio dropped down from a tree with a big smile. Tomato seeds dotted his hair. "The direction you're looking for? *It is the east.* Juliet, pleasure to be sneaking around with you. But, er, I'm not sure I understand your costume. Are you a tangerine?"

"*Juliet is the sun*," Romeo said.

"Oh!" Mercutio said. He helped Juliet to her feet. "*Arise, fair sun.* Let's go stop Tybalt, for the sake of Verona and sensitive noses everywhere!"

CHAPTER NINETEEN
FIDDLING WITH THE RIDDLE OF TYBALT

"Stop looking at me," Juliet said.

"You stop looking at *me*!" Romeo snapped back.

"You were looking at me first."

"You're in front of me! It's not my fault you're in the way of my eyes."

"Maybe I should've turned you in when I had the chance. You'd be in the Capulet dungeons right now being tortured."

"I tried the Instead-Stix. After that, torture sounds pleasant."

Becca sighed, and next to her she heard Sam grind his teeth.

Juliet and Romeo had bickered as they passed the bakery.

They had fumed as they passed the farmers' market.

They had been quarreling, squabbling, and arguing up and down the dark streets of Verona, and Becca was nearing the end of her Instead-Stix rope.

"Are we there yet?" she asked Mercutio.

"I *told* you, we'll get there when we get there!"

Becca blinked. It seemed even good-natured Mercutio was getting annoyed by the feuding Miss Capulet and Mr. Montague. They couldn't get to the apothecary soon enough!

"What is an apothecary, anyway?" Becca asked.

Mercutio looked at her in surprise. "You really *are* from far away."

"Something like that," Sam said.

"Apothecaries learn about different plants

and herbs and such things," Mercutio said, sniffling a bit. "They mix them to make medicines and potions, including perfumes." He sniffed again. "I may need some medicine myself. My nose is still itching from the last time I was around your pup."

THHHHHBBBBBTTTTT!

Becca turned in time to see Romeo make a raspberry at Juliet, who immediately crossed her eyes at him. Mercutio picked up the pace.

After two more lefts and then a right, Becca was about to tell Juliet to stop repeating everything Romeo said, when Mercutio *finally* came to a halt. "We're here!"

The apothecary shop looked like a witch's cottage—or what Becca would have imagined a witch's cottage to look like. The window was so filled with bottles and flasks in all different

colors and sizes that she couldn't see anything

in the shop itself. There was no way of telling if Tybalt and his hostage were in there or not.

"Tybalt's been renting it for cheap because our apothecary's out of town for a while," Juliet whispered. "Apparently some big disaster stank up a castle all the way in Denmark, and they wrote to people all over Europe to ask for help."

"It's quiet," Mercutio said, peering in. "I don't see any light inside."

Becca in no way wanted to enter the shop. Its eerie silence reminded her of a tomb. More specifically, the Egyptian tomb where Mal and Cal had their very first encounter with a mummy. Mal and Cal had bravely ventured through, though. Becca gritted her teeth. If her fictional characters could withstand the silence and dark, then so could she!

"THE MUMMY HAD THE INNOCENT PUP IN ITS BANDAGED CLUTCHES. MAL AND CAL APPROACHED CAREFULLY, DETERMINED TO SAVE THE PET FROM A WORLD OF REALLY DRY BONES." —*THE ASTOUNDING ADVENTURES OF MAL & CAL WORTHY*, ISSUE #31.

WORDS BY BECCA DEED, ILLUSTRATIONS BY KYLE WORD.

"Is there a back door?" Sam asked.

"Pretty sure it's just this one," Juliet said.

Then from inside there came a faint whine. It could have just been the wind . . . but it also could have been a dog in trouble.

Becca stepped closer to the window. "Did you hear that?"

"I heard something," Sam said, and Romeo nodded.

As carefully as she could, Becca pressed her ear against the wooden door. There it was again—a low whimper.

Becca jerked her head away. "Rufus is in there!"

"We have to be smart about this," Mercutio warned. "We can't just open the door. Tybalt might be trying to lure us into a trap."

"You're right." Becca turned to Juliet. "You're his cousin, right? Maybe you can reason with him. Call him out here so we can separate him from Rufus."

Juliet had finally stopped making faces at Romeo and now looked very serious. "I can try," she said doubtfully. "But Tybalt is not known for being reasonable."

Romeo snorted. "I'll say."

"Stop agreeing with me!"

"Fight later," Becca said, snapping her fingers. "Rescue now."

"I'll try," Juliet said again. She knocked on the door. "Tybalt? Cousin? Are you in there?"

No answer.

"I think I know how to get back at the Montagues," she said in a deeper voice. "We can beat them once and for all!"

But if Tybalt was inside, he wasn't convinced. The shop remained as quiet and still as school on a snow day.

"Any other ideas?" Romeo asked.

Luckily, Becca had one.

"I do?" Becca said.

"She does?" said Sam.

Juliet and Mercutio looked at them quizzically.

"We'll explain later," Sam said.

"Shh," Becca said. "I have an idea?"

You're supposed to. That's how the story should work. Has it not come to you yet?

"I . . . don't think so."

Okay. Here's a hint: *Achoo!*

"Gesundheit."

No. That was the hint.

Becca thought for a moment. She looked at Mercutio, who was still standing at the window.

"Ohhhhhh," she said. A story started to come to her—and an idea of what a hero might do. "Do any of you think you can get that window open? Quietly?" Becca asked in a whisper.

Juliet stepped forward. "Having the nurse I

do has made me an expert in all things sneaky," she said. She pulled a brass hairpin shaped like a shining sun from her head. Next she found a tiny gap in the window and slowly worked it open.

"Sam, do you have any of Mrs. W.'s cookies left?"

"Just one." He reached into his pocket and handed it to her.

"Thanks," she said. "Mercutio, face the window, please."

"As you command!"

"Hold still," she said and placed the cookie on the sill. She cleared her throat and half whispered, "Rufus, treat!"

Mercutio's eyes widened. "But . . . I'm allergi— ACHOO!"

A thunderstorm of spit and snot geysered out of his mouth and nose and into the apothecary shop.

"Why's it raining?" came Tybalt's voice from inside. "Is there a leak? Why's it so sticky and . . .

EEEEEEEEEEEEEEEEEEEEEEEEEEEEEEWWWWWW!"

Becca listened in satisfaction as Tybalt—who

bathed in flowery water every day, who tweezed his mustache into shape twice a week, who wore more cologne than most royal families— came tearing out the door, frantically swiping snot off himself with one hand while gripping a rope in the other.

And at the end of *that* rope was the very tied-up, very slobbery Rufus.

CHAPTER TWENTY
NOSING YOUR WAY TO VICTORY

"Rufus!" Becca cried.

"Becca!" Sam said joyfully.

"Tybalt!" Juliet said angrily.

"Juliet," Tybalt said, hurt.

"Steve!" Mercutio exclaimed. Everyone
turned to stare at him. "Oh, are we only yelling
one another's names?" He shrugged and
unhooked his sword. "Doesn't matter, I guess.
En garde!"

Tybalt's angry eyes narrowed at Sam. "You!" he growled. "You're the one who stained my doublet! And unless my eyes deceive me—that's Romeo Montague standing next to you!"

Sam crossed his arms. "And you stole our dog and my sister's backpack. We want them back!"

"Yeah?" Tybalt sneered. "Or what?"

"Or we'll make all your perfume smell like wet dog," Becca said.

"You wouldn't dare," Tybalt snarled, but he took a small step back in surprise.

That step was all Becca needed.

"Get him!" she shouted.

They all rushed Tybalt, but his sword was out half a blink later. Becca skidded to a halt. She really, really hoped Rufus wouldn't

think the sword was some extra-fun shiny stick.

"That's an antique!" Tybalt roared as his sword flew from him. His hand shot out, and he grabbed Sam's arm. "I shall have all your heads! Starting with his."

From his doublet, he pulled out a hidden dagger and held it to Sam's throat.

The world suddenly became very, very still.

"Stop, Tybalt!" Juliet yelled as she brandished a rotten tomato. It had patches of fuzzy white mold on it. "Unless you want your last clean suit to look like it was finger painted, let Samikins go!"

Tybalt eyed the juicy weapon warily. He glanced down at Sam's head, then slowly back up to the tomato aimed at him.

With a nod, he pulled his dagger away from Sam's neck and put it back into his jacket . . . then whipped out the biggest, drippiest, most intimidating tomato Becca had ever laid eyes on.

"Easy, Juliet," Tybalt said. "You've already had one dress ruined tonight. Do you really want to make it two? Just answer me this: Were you part of the tomato plot all along?"

Juliet's lower lip stuck out. "Are you really accusing me of working with the Montagues?" she asked. "I fought next to you when they attacked! But you kidnapped an innocent animal who has nothing to do with the pizza war!"

"All's fair in perfume and war," Tybalt said. "I owe it to the world to share my beautiful scents even if a puppy tail or two gets hurt in the process."

"*Beautiful scents?*" Juliet shrieked. "Your cologne could knock out a mule! It could knock out a mule with its nose buried in mud! It could shock a dead mule back to life and then kill it again with the stench!!"

Tybalt's face turned red. "Don't you insult my fragrant masterpiece!" he shouted, and whipped the tomato at her.

TYBALT'S VIOLENT VIOLET

SPLOOOSH!!!

Becca screamed and ducked her head as little bits of tomato guts sprinkled down on her. As she wiped tomato seeds from her eyes, she dreaded what she would see—but the scene wasn't what she expected.

Juliet still stood, dress spotless, while Romeo lay at her feet, tomato plastered all over his face. While the rest of them had stood still, Romeo had acted—and taken the tomato for Juliet. The impact of the flying fruit had knocked him out cold.

And in the moment of surprise, Tybalt bolted.

"Don't let him escape!" Becca yelled. "I still need my backpack."

Mercutio and Sam sped after him while Becca scooped up more tomatoes from the sidewalk. By the time she had an armload, Tybalt had put Sam in a headlock, and her stepbrother's face had become a pale shade of green. She wasn't sure how much longer he could take being so close to Tybalt's flowery and deadly fumes.

Picking out the blackest, squishiest tomato, she drew her arm back—

Only to have it caught in an iron grip.

"STOP!!"

CHAPTER TWENTY-ONE
COLLABORATE AND LISTEN

Becca twisted around to see a woman with a steel-colored bun pulled so tight that it looked painful.

"Nurse?" Juliet said, mouth hanging open.

"Who?" Sam said, eyeing the newcomer.

"Oh, er," Juliet said, "everyone, this is Nurse. She's my nanny."

"That's right, I am," Nurse said, "and I intend to see that you turn out well, no matter what nonsense you may get into. Everyone, drop what you're doing this instant!"

Becca dropped her tomato.

Mercutio dropped his sword.

Juliet dropped Romeo's wrist, which she'd been checking for a pulse.

The nurse pointed a square finger at Tybalt. "You, too, Tybalt Kenneth Fiore Rudolfo Capulet!"

Tybalt shifted uncomfortably, then finally let go of Sam, who dropped to the street.

"That's better," Nurse said, crossing

her arms. "You may have your own perfumery, but you're not head of the Capulets yet! Go home—you're grounded for a week! And for goodness' sake, take a bath before that perfume puts your whole family in a coma."

"But that's Romeo Montague and his minions!" Tybalt said. "The Montagues stole our dough recipe! I was only trying to stand up and do some good for the Capulets."

"Nonsense," Nurse said crisply. "You're only blaming the Montagues because you can't figure out a new perfume recipe. Maybe you can come up with a new one while you're grounded. Now, *go home.*"

Tybalt opened his mouth to argue again, but he got a look from the nurse that could've split lumber. He lowered his head and his shoulders drooped.

"Wait a second!" Becca squeaked, and she shook as everyone looked at her. "Tybalt also took a purple backpack. Where is it?"

Tybalt mumbled something.

"Speak up, Tybalt," Nurse ordered. "Or it's *two* weeks, *and* I take away your perfume kit!"

"It's in the apothecary's," Tybalt said sullenly.

Becca went back inside, careful to avoid the mucus puddles left over from Mercutio's sneezing. Purple straps peeked out from behind the apothecary's counter. She hurried over.

Zipping her bag open, she saw with relief that *Romeo and Juliet* was still in there. She ran back outside just in time to see Tybalt slink away.

Nurse, Mercutio, and Juliet were all gathered around Romeo, while Sam was carefully checking Rufus for injuries.

"Did you get the book?" he whispered.

"Yeah," she said. "Is Roo okay?"

"I think so," Sam said. "His nose is a little bit runny, but what do you expect after an hour being locked up with Tybalt's bad cologne? He deserves lots of extra treats for his bravery."

WOOF! Roo's tail gave a small wag.

"I'm sure we can convince Steve to get an extra bag." She scratched Rufus's ears, and the big fluff pile let out a relaxed grunt.

"Hey," Sam said. "Did you just refer to my dad—Stephen R. Danielson III—as Steve?"

"Did I?" Becca said, pausing midscratch to look at Sam. "I guess I did."

Sam grinned, and Becca felt her daydreams of flowers and grass skirts finally disappear.

"I'm happy you're okay, Roo," Becca said,

changing the subject. She kissed the puppy on his big, wet, sniffly nose. She was rewarded with a SLURP across her face.

The three family members quickly hurried over to Romeo. Juliet was still cradling his head in her hands.

"You took a tomato for me," Juliet said softly. "And we had such a lovely conversation about pizza. But . . . you're a Montague." She sighed. *"Romeo, Romeo . . . Wherefore art thou Romeo?"*

"He's right there," Sam said.

Wherefore doesn't mean
where. It means *why*.

"Ohhhh."

"Sam," Juliet said, looking up, "I still think you're great, and I want to thank you for your bravery in dealing with Tybalt, but I . . . I think I need to take a little while to figure out my feelings. I'm sorry."

"No, no, quite all right," Sam said, turning redder than an exploding ketchup factory on Mars.

"But Romeo . . . if you were anyone else . . ." Juliet shook her head sadly.

"Nonsense," Nurse cut in. "So what if your families have been fighting for years? Doesn't mean you have to keep doing it. If you ask me, all of Verona has been acting like children since its pizza ingredients were stolen. And it's all the Narrator's fault!"

Becca's and Sam's heads whipped toward her.

"The Narrator?" Becca said. "Do you know anything about him—or her?"

Nurse narrowed her eyes at them. "So you know the Narrator, then. . . . Curious."

"No, we don't—not personally—but we'd like to," Sam chimed in.

"Then I'm afraid you're asking the wrong person. I only know that the Narrator likes to stir up trouble."

A thought popped into Becca's head, and she whirled around to face a wide-eyed Sam.

"Do you think—" she began.

"—that the Narrator stole the cheese and the dough recipe?" Sam finished grimly. "Yeah, I do. He seems to enjoy chaos."

Becca turned her eyes upward, waiting for the Narrator to defend its honor.

"Pssst, I know you're there!" she whispered.

There was no answer, and there

wouldn't be one coming. It
was a question for another
time, in another book.

"Look!" Juliet said excitedly. "Romeo's
moving!"

"Urrrf," Romeo said, stirring slightly.
"What happened? Why is it dark? Tybalt
blinded me!"

"No, silly, it's just tomato chunks that
have crusted to your eyelashes," Juliet said.
The nurse handed her a cloth, and she wiped
Romeo's eyes clean.

He blinked once, twice, and then stared
deeply into Juliet's eyes.

"Uh, are you all right?" Sam asked.

"Did I love till now?" Romeo practically
sighed, not breaking eye contact with Juliet.

"Forswear it, sight: I never saw true beauty till this night."

Juliet turned bright pink—the pink of a sunburned flamingo swimming in grapefruit juice. She gave him an earsplitting smile.

"Wow," Sam whispered to Becca. "He really *is* a poet. And he didn't even—"

"Don't," Becca said, clamping her hand over his mouth. "The tomato hit on the head must have knocked some poetry into him!"

"Will you go to the Lotsa-Rella Ball with me tomorrow?" Romeo asked.

Juliet's face was now magenta. "I'd love to." She beamed.

Becca grinned at her stepbrother. "This is it! We can go home now! Thank you, Nurse. . . . Nurse?" She looked around the Verona square, but the nurse was nowhere to be seen. "Wow. Is she a superhero?"

"Definitely," Mercutio said. "I've seen her cape."

CHAPTER TWENTY-TWO
ALL'S WELL THAT ENDS— SORRY, WRONG PLAY

Juliet helped Romeo to his feet, and even though he swayed a little, Becca thought he'd be okay.

"Thank you," Juliet said to Becca and Sam. "I'm not sure why you decided to get involved in an ancient family war, but I'm glad you did."

"We didn't exactly decide to," Sam said. "But I'm glad we helped."

"Me, too," Becca said, and scratched Rufus's ears. "Roo, too."

Woof! he agreed.

"I'll miss all of you," Mercutio said, a tear coming to his eye. He took out a handkerchief and blew his nose with the sound of a hundred geese singing opera. "Although my nose won't miss your dog."

"Either way," Sam said to Romeo and Juliet, "the two of you can help your families make peace no matter what."

"I agree," Juliet said. "If we can get them talking, convince them that they didn't steal each other's stuff, well, it's a start. If a Montague and a Capulet can be friends, who knows what else we can change?"

Panic rose in Becca's chest. "Er—*just* friends?" she tried to ask casually.

"Boyfriend and girlfriend," Juliet amended.

And this time it was Romeo's turn to be pink.

"Although"—Juliet looked at Romeo—"now that I think of it, it would be nice if we could attend our first party together in matching costumes."

"Er, I really don't think that's necessary—"

Juliet snapped her fingers. "I know! We'll take your cloak and cut it out in little stars!"

"Stars?" Romeo said uncertainly. "I don't know, that doesn't sound very . . ."

Sam prodded him in the side and leaned down to whisper to him. "Here's some dating advice. Learn to go with the flow a little bit. Compromise. If it's love, she'll do the same for you. Who knows? You might even like it."

Romeo pondered for a moment and nodded. "I guess I can give it a try."

"Wise choice," Becca said, and smiled at Sam.

It turned out her stepbrother
wasn't so terrible after all. Only
just a little bit horrible. "Good luck!"

And after one last farewell belly
rub for Rufus, Romeo and Juliet walked off
together, hand in hand.

"Well," Mercutio said, sweeping them a bow.
"I think this is where I make my exit. I have an
appointment with Queen Mab."

"Who?" Sam asked.

"*She is the fairies' midwife, and she comes in
shape no bigger than an agate stone,*" Mercutio

said, hopping onto a barrel. "Also, she's my cat, who is in need of feeding. Farewell!"

"Well," Becca said as they watched Mercutio's receding back, "at last we can turn that final page."

Sam handed her backpack to her, and she quickly opened it. Even though it had been through several tomato fights, her pencils were still there, along with her notebook, and, of course, the large leather book with the words *Romeo and Juliet* on the cover.

Carefully, she laid it on the ground. "I hope this works. Ready?"

Sam grabbed Rufus's collar. "You better believe it."

Becca took a deep breath . . . and flipped to the last page.

"Woo-hoo!" Sam yelled just as loudly as he

did while watching basketball tournaments.

"MVP Becca!"

"What's that mean?"

"Most valuable player." Sam frowned. "Though, in this case I guess it should MVR— most valuable reader!"

Becca smiled. Perhaps Sam could be useful sometimes . . . when he wasn't playing pranks or almost turning the world's most famous love story into *Sam and Juliet*.

"Hey," she said as she reached to grab onto Rufus's collar. "Do you want to read the last line with me?"

He nodded. "Sure."

And together, they read: "*For never was a story of more woe, than this of Juliet and her Romeo.*"

Verona shimmered, trembled, and vanished in a tornado of words.

CHAPTER TWENTY-THREE
IF I NEVER SEE A TOMATO AGAIN . . .

Kyle's living room reappeared around them, shimmery at first, as though they were seeing it through a bubble. Then there was a *pop!* and the world came into focus—along with Kyle, Halley, and Kyle's baby brother, Gabe. Or Gross Gabe, as Kyle never failed to call him. The light coming in the windows was just the way they'd left it, like all of their time in Verona had been only a few seconds.

"You made it!" Kyle and Becca both said at once.

"Where were you?" Sam and Halley asked together.

"That was crazy," everyone said in unison.

"Did you get sucked into a book, too?" asked Becca.

"Yes! Where did your magic trap book take you?" Kyle said.

Becca took a deep breath and gave them a brief overview of what had just happened to them.

"Whoa," Kyle said. "I don't know if that sounds better or worse than a library full of skulls, an insane king who likes dropping people in soup, and a sad prince in a castle that smells like a pizza-with-everything left under a couch for a year."

Becca thought both sounded pretty bad. Or pretty exciting, depending on how you looked at it.

"Hey, Roodly Roo!" Halley said, bending down to deliver a flurry of pets to Rufus's head. "I bet you had a tough time, huh, pups?"

"He'll probably never eat a tomato again," Sam said.

Kyle raised an eyebrow.

"We'll tell you all about it," Sam added. "In fact, we should definitely, absolutely all sit down and go over whatever just happened in more detail, and maybe figure out what to do next."

Rufus and Gabe started rolling around together, as if getting sucked into four-hundred-year-old plays was as much part of their daily life as eating breakfast.

"Now that that's over," Becca said to Sam, "I can finally return that library book. Then Kyle and I can send in the fee for our contest entry. I hope I get there in time." Although staying in

Hawaii and ditching everyone else forever was no longer part of her plan if they won.

"I can run it to the library for you," Sam said. "I'm fast."

"Okay." Becca nodded. "As long as you promise this won't involve any water buckets or tomatoes."

"Ugh," Sam said. "I bet we both picked up a tomato allergy after all that. Anyway, even if the library's closed, I . . . have a key."

"You what?" Becca said. "Why?"

"Well, sixth grade has a community service requirement, and I thought volunteering at the library might be cool. The librarians have always been super nice to me." He shrugged. "If my basketball career doesn't work out, I think I might want to be one when I grow up. Actually, even if my basketball career *does* work out, I still want to be a librarian."

Becca smiled and shook her head. "Wow, Sam. Between this and being eaten by a book, I'm not sure what's surprised me more today. Thanks."

Still smiling, Becca turned to look at Kyle, who looked like he'd actually *enjoyed* the conversation he'd had with Halley. The surprises just kept coming.

Becca decided to take charge, like the Narrator would have. "First, let's pack these books up and ship 'em back. Or bury them. Something."

Looking around, she spotted *Romeo and Juliet* lying on the floor a few feet away. She reached out a hand very slowly, brushing a corner of the book and yanking her hand back. When nothing happened, she picked it up. Something caught her eye. "Hey, wait a minute. . . ."

There was a piece of paper stuck in the book

that hadn't been there before, and she tugged it out.

"Um, does anyone else want to read this?"

Kyle shook his head very fast.

"I'll do it," Halley said. Becca only felt relief as she handed her the note.

"*Dear Reader,*" Halley read, rolling her eyes as she said it, "*I hope you enjoyed your first thrilling and educational expedition with the Get Lost Book Club. No doubt you already miss the escape our club can give you from ordinary life. Don't worry, though. This was just the first of many adventures to come.*"

"Oh no," Kyle said. "Absolutely not. No. I'm never opening one of those old books again."

"I don't know if I'll ever open *any* book again," Becca said. "What if I got nabbed by a math textbook or a train schedule?"

"I have some *great* ideas for future *Mal & Cal Worthy* adventures, though," Kyle said to Becca.

"Me, too!" she replied. "If we don't win the Storyland contest this year, we'll definitely win it next year. But let's talk about that after we've hurled these books into the sun."

"Yeah," Kyle agreed. "I mean, I still want to go to Hawaii eventually, but *Hamlet* was pretty exciting even though I didn't leave my living room. Not"—he quickly added—"that I ever want to get lost in a book again!"

"I hope you've all been having a good time," Mrs. Word said, walking into the living room with cinnamon-stained hands. "Wow, Kyle, is that *Hamlet*?" she said. "I didn't realize you were studying Shakespeare. You like it?"

Becca saw Kyle and Halley exchange a look.

"Yeah," Kyle said through what sounded like clenched teeth. "It was gripping."

"Captivating," Halley said.

Becca smiled. "One of those stories you feel like you're right in the middle of."

"You can almost smell it," Sam added.

Mrs. Word smiled delightedly. "You three are all welcome to stay for dinner if you'd like. Mr. W. said it'll be ready soon. He's got a big pot of tomato soup bubbling."

Becca's stomach lurched. She put her hands on her stomach, trying to let it know she wouldn't subject it to any more Instead-Stix and marinara sauce. But it didn't help that Kyle was telling Gabe that tomatoes were actually *yummy.*

"Uh," Sam said, grabbing his basketball off the carpet. "I'd love to, but I have to . . . write

that essay about, um, carpentry. Becca, you
need that library book returned, right? I'll
grab that and run over to the library first. I bid
thee—I mean, have a good night!" He made his
exit as if he were being pursued by a bear.

"More for the rest of you," Kyle's mom said,
smiling. "It should be almost ready—" She
suddenly stopped talking and blinked once.
"What's that awful smell?"

DEAR READER,

Congratulations: You, too, made
it through the perils of the book!
You followed Becca, Sam, and the brave Rufus on their
strange, perilous, and eye-opening journey through the
world of *Romeo and Juliet*. You, as they did, found out
new things, watched other characters change, and maybe
started to understand a little more about the world.

As with every journey and every story, some
questions are answered at the end, but some remain
unanswered. Where did the Narrator hide the stolen
cheese and dough recipe? Who is this Ophelia, Romeo's
mysterious long-distance poetry teacher? And what
strange adventures did Halley and Kyle have while Becca
and Sam were stuck in Verona?

As with most questions, the answers can be found
within a book. If you're brave enough to dive back
in. William Shakespeare wrote a great many plays,
including one called *Hamlet*. Kingly treason, ghosts,
skulls, tights . . . Perhaps nothing as dangerous as
Romeo's poetry, but some of it comes close.

There are so many more books to explore. If you
want more answers, and more important, if you want to
find new questions to ask, that's the best place to look.

Sincerely,

The Narrator

LISTEN TO THE NARRATOR!

SOLVE MORE MYSTERIES IN THIS BOOK

Available now wherever books are sold!

Do you have an eye for epic quests?
Enjoy spending time in your imagination?
Want to go on an adventure?

Then sign up for the

STORYLAND YOUNG STORYTELLER CONTEST**

Enter your

SHORT STORY	NOVELLA
POEM	NOVEL
COMIC BOOK	EPIC

and win an

ALL-EXPENSES-PAID TRIP TO OUR HAWAIIAN LOCATION!

For more information, register online, and you'll receive the Storyland Young Storyteller Contest Guidelines in the mail.*

*By participating in the contest, entrant warrants and represents that his/her entry is original to the entrant, has not been previously published or won any award, and does not contain any material that would violate or infringe upon the rights of any third party, including copyrights (including, without limitation, copyrighted images or footage), trademarks, or rights of privacy or publicity.

Please note that by entering the contest, you are also signing up for the Get Lost Book Club, founded by the most wonderful and splendid Narrator of all time.

**Sorry, kids; the Narrator is a jerk, and this contest is not real. He would still like to read your stories, though. Please send them, along with any complaints about his treachery, to the address located in this book—if you can find it (Hint: it's on the copyright page, near a certain book curse).

ABOUT THE AUTHOR

M.E. CASTLE is a New York City-raised writer and actor living in Washington, DC. He is the author of the beloved Clone Chronicles, which introduced the world to Fisher Bas and his clones, a flying pig, and a large supporting cast of robots, aliens, and a very proper talking toaster. When not writing, he can be found performing the works of Shakespeare onstage, which has given him the expertise necessary to create this utterly scholarly and serious work.

ABOUT THE ILLUSTRATOR

DANIEL JENNEWEIN has been drawing since kindergarten, where he could mainly be found drawing skulls and hooks, to the irritation of some adults. He works as a freelance illustrator and art director in Frankfurt. His picture books include *Is Your Buffalo Ready for Kindergarten?* (written by Audrey Vernick, 2010), *Teach Your Buffalo to Play Drums* (written by Audrey Vernick, 2011), and *Chick-o-Saurus Rex* (written by Lenore Jennewein, 2013).
danieljennewein.com

ACKNOWLEDGMENTS

I have been fortunate enough in my life to not only write goofy, whimsical books as a job, but to perform Shakespeare live on stage as a job as well. Of all my enthusiastically geeky interests, Shakespeare is hard to top. Stepping into a playing space and embodying characters from and for all time, speaking words committed to paper when the printing press was scarcely more than a century old and reigned as the cutting edge of idea dissemination, is an experience profound and thrilling enough that I couldn't possibly give this sentence an ending that would do it justice.

It was that deep fondness in my heart that

led to these books, and the odd adventures of the characters within. They aren't severe departures from Shakespearean tendencies, either. His plays *are* full of silly jokes and "lowbrow" humor. They *are*, for the most part, straightforward stories with big, easily relatable themes. And they *are* entirely capable of being appreciated—and understood—by young audiences. It's my hope that the Fakespeare tales will be enjoyed both as stories in their own right and as a way to tell young readers not to be afraid of Shakespeare.

I must thank the excellent people at Paper Lantern, in particular Kamilla Benko and Lexa Hillyer, the latter of whom helped with this project while preparing to have and subsequently caring for an entirely other tiny human, a task I can't conceive the dauntingness of. I also extend heartfelt thanks to the good people at Macmillan, without whom you could read this book only if I printed it out, walked up, and handed it to you. My editor (and publisher of Imprint)

Erin Stein, editorial assistant Nicole Otto, creative director

Natalie C. Sousa, associate marketing director Kathryn

Little, publicist Kelsey Marrujo, senior production manager

Raymond Ernesto Colón, and production editor Ilana Worrell.

I also want to thank those who led me down the path

to Shakespeare: Woody Howard, one of my first acting

teachers and the subject of this book's dedication, and

Paul Moser, whose Shakespeare acting course was the

centerpiece of my acting training. I also want to toss

some thanks to the good people of the Adirondack

Shakespeare Company who keep hiring me to act in

their productions even after getting to know me.

As always, thanks to all of my friends for giving me

someone to discuss these cool things with, my mother and

sister for taking time out of doing great things themselves

to cheer me on, and a lady named Andrea whom I asked

to dance a few years ago and, to my great fortune, haven't

yet trod on the toes of enough to end that dance.